Bill Doolin: American Outlaw

Bill Doolin: American Outlaw

Bill Brooks

FIVE STAR

A part of Gale, Cengage Learning

GALE
CENGAGE Learning

Farmington Hills, Mich • San Francisco • New York • Waterville, Maine
Meriden, Conn • Mason, Ohio • Chicago

Five Star™ Publishing, a part of Cengage Learning, Inc.

LIBRARY OF CONGRESS CATALOGING-IN-PUBLICATION DATA

Names: Brooks, Bill, 1943– author.
Title: Bill Doolin : American outlaw / by Bill Brooks.
Description: First edition. | Waterville, Maine : Five Star, a part of Cengage Learning, Inc. [2016]
Identifiers: LCCN 2016003813| ISBN 9781432832261 (hardcover) | ISBN 1432832263 (hardcover)
Subjects: | GSAFD: Western stories.
Classification: LCC PS3552.R65863 B55 2016 | DDC 813/.54—dc23
LC record available at http://lccn.loc.gov/2016003813

First Edition. First Printing: August 2016
Find us on Facebook– https://www.facebook.com/FiveStarCengage
Visit our website– http://www.gale.cengage.com/fivestar/
Contact Five Star™ Publishing at FiveStar@cengage.com

Printed in the United States of America
1 2 3 4 5 6 7 20 19 18 17 16

Once again for Diane, who makes everything better.

AUTHOR'S NOTE

This is a work of fiction based on real people and real events, though the author did take the liberty of fictionalizing some of the less important events and conversations, hopefully without detracting from the important elements of their story.

THE LEE BROTHERS OR DEATH IN A HAYFIELD

Dexter, Texas, 1885

Wind exalted through the hayfield as hot and insistent as the Devil's breath. The Lee boys had run themselves square into a trap. Hunkered down hoping the posse would not espy them, they were as rankled as a pair of scurvy dogs.

"I ain't gone a surrender and be hanged for killing those law-dogs," Pink said to his brother Jim.

"Me either. Fuck 'em."

"So we stay and fight?"

"Don't reckon we got no choice."

"How many you reckon they be?"

"Too many."

"Goddamn," Pink said, and spat juice from the wad of plug tobacco balled inside his cheek. Levered his Winchester forgetting that there was already a shell in the chamber and watched it spit out the brass cartridge. He reached down and picked it up and rubbed dirt off it.

"Daresn't waste any," he said.

"We'll need every damn one we got."

"How come you reckon they found us?"

"Luck or accident, I guess it was."

"You think it's Heck and them?"

"I don't know who else it'd be. You know how Heck is when he gets onto you: like a dog on a pork chop bone."

"I reckon the pork chop this time is us."

"You see them?"

"Can't see shit, 'less I stand up. I do that I'll get my head blowed off."

Again the call to surrender: "You boys toss down your weapons and come out with your hands in the air."

"Yeah, that's Heck Thomas, all right. I'd know that sumbitch's voice anywhere."

"You come out we won't kill you," the voice said. "We got this whole hayfield surrounded. Otherwise . . . well, you don't want to know otherwise."

"What you think, little brother?"

"I think we're dead either way. Bullet or rope, either way you die and ain't none of it no good."

"I reckon I'd as soon get shot as to strangulate at the end of some rope with the rubes standing around watching me do an air jig, some butcher selling candy to them while we put on a show."

"Mama and them," Pink said.

"I've seen men hang. They soil themselves. I couldn't bear to see our own mama watch us die like that, could you?"

"Hey, Heck!"

"What is it, boys?"

"I reckon Pink and me just as soon say fuck you and them with you. We're not going to let you hang us."

"Last chance. These boys is hungry and tired and want to go home to their wives. Don't know how much longer I can hold 'em at bay. They're hot for blood, Pink."

"No. Want us, you come in and get us if any of you all got the nerve."

The brothers glanced at each other, grinned, levered their Winchesters again, and leapt up firing at men they could not see hunkered down in the tall stems of endless green grasses that stood nearly chest high. Grass that would go through its second cutting and be rolled into bales and stored into mows for the feeding of livestock through the harsh winter months.

Soon as they jumped to their feet, they were instantly scythed down by a slantwise storm of bullets that split the air and ripped into their bodies with thuds and snaps, clipping belt buckles and buttons, splintering bone and ripping flesh. It hurt worse than either of them could imagine, those bullets of the lawmen.

"Oh, hell, oh, hell!" Pink said as the flames of pain rummaged through him, breaking a wrist, shattering a shoulder, smashing a knee. He saw part of his brother's jaw torn away by a round that left him a bloody half face exposing white jawbone and teeth, the gore spewing out of what had been Jim's mouth, a cranberry-red offal.

Almost as quickly, a bullet ripped into Pink's groin and exited out his tailbone and folded him inward. He cussed the pain, his dumb luck, the luck of the unseen shooter. The bullets shrieked through the grasses and found their flesh again and again, the crack of Winchesters sounding like splintering boards.

Then someone shouted, "Cease firing!" and a great yawing silence enveloped the hayfield, a soundless expectancy that seemed to search out the shooters.

Heck Thomas and his posse stood with Winchesters thrown into their shoulders, waiting, fingers on triggers, eyes slighted down the length of blued barrels breathing smoke, a tingling in the blood that was both frightful and pleasurable.

"You reckon they're dead, Heck?"

"I reckon maybe they are."

"I seen one's head explode," someone said.

"Pink or Jim?" Heck called.

No answer.

"Let's move in slowly," he said and the posse advanced through the grasses until they came upon the bodies of Jim and Pink Lee who lay close together, one face down, the other face up, Pink's face a frozen grimace as if the groin wound was still hurting him.

"They're dead as shit," someone said.

"That they surely are," Heck replied, then ordered that the wagon be brought in, the bodies loaded into it and hauled back to town. Those boys had decent reward money on their heads and Heck would collect it and divide it among the posse as he'd always done. Then once more he would ride home to waiting wife and children that was as far away from the silent blood-filled scene as it could be.

He would sleep in his own bed but more and more without a wife willing to absolve him of his sins. Warm wind would blow through an open window, lifting and dropping the white curtains in a sad dance, and he would ask himself was it all worth it—the life he chose to lead.

Though discontent with intimacies, his wife would dutifully cook a meal for them, padding about in bare feet dressed in only a thin nightgown through which he could see the shape of her, the fine curves and turns of her body, while he sat at the kitchen table and smoked his pipe and nursed a cup of Arbuckle coffee, frustrated. She would ask him again to seek other employment. But his answer was always the same.

"It's the work I do and the work I'm good at and there will never be a shortage of jobs for men like me and that mad Dane Chris Madsen and old Bill Tilghman. The country needs us."

She would sigh and bring him his dinner and sit across from him as he ate and he would try not to think too much of what he lacked in way of a marriage compared to other men. His small children would climb on him like he was a wild bear that needed to be tamed. He loved them children terrible bad.

"I need you to stay home with us, Heck," she would say icily. Then when he would not respond, she would change the subject and say something like, "I wished it would rain soon," or, "Will you read me some Byron later?" They loved the poetry of Byron.

"Yes, I will," he would say.

And the killing and bloodshed would for a time be put aside, as say a book just read is put on a shelf to be forgotten for a time. By the new miracle of electric light, he would later read to her a favorite passage, hoping to stir in her some passion:

We sat down and wept by the waters
Of Babel, and thought of the day
When our foe, in the hue of his slaughters,
Made Salem's high places his prey;
And ye, oh her desolate daughters!
Were scattered all weeping away

But the passion she withheld no matter how hard he tried and only one thing would satisfy her, the one thing he could not give her and another day and night would pass between them until it was time for him to ride off again in search of new murderers, rapists, and thieves.

Chapter 1

Doolin traveled the back roads up and down. The music of his travel: the clop of hooves upon hardpan, creak of saddle leather, and jingle of bit was hardly a symphony except to a man with empty pockets and grand dreams, which his were.

He'd left a woman in a warm bed and travelled for six days straight and already his bones and blood ached mightily for her. His soul felt like an empty beer glass waiting to be refilled, his sexual ache a longing he could not otherwise fill.

He had known hard times and lonely before, but nothing felt as lonely as knowing love and not having it at hand.

He went along, one hand holding the reins, and wondered why he did it at all. Why can't you be like other men and content with any sort of job? It don't have to be robbing trains and banks. It was an old argument he held with himself every time he set forth toward a new piece of dark business.

He'd carried on this little debate about each leaving their place in Lawson. Well, her pap's place, for they were, as he liked to prefer it, between domiciles.

Her pap was a bona fide preaching man, white collar and thin-soled shoes and a holy book that weighed two pounds at least. Her pap found a solace in that large book that escaped Doolin altogether. So much of it was a mystery to him that he simply gave up trying to figure it.

He envisioned her now as he rode along the road with its arabesque pattern of sunlight and tree limbs. This time of year the leaves were tumbling earthward like shot birds, with wings stiff and curled. Gold birds, red birds, brown birds.

She stood naked in the moonlight of his memory. He wondered still what she ever saw in him, a rough old cob with pinched and puckered scars. She exclaimed that he was a beautiful man, to which he would laugh and say, "They is nothing pretty about me except my dreams, Edith Anne."

Just thinking about her caused his groin to stir till he forced himself to think about those who were to be waiting for him.

Something didn't feel good about it, but onward he rode because of his empty pockets.

He built himself a cigarette of Bull Durham tobacco and smoking papers and rolled it neatly between blunted fingers. Then found a match somewhere in one of his pockets and struck it with a thumbnail and cupped the flame to the end of his shuck, blowing it out when he exhaled his first drag of smoke.

He didn't much care to harness himself to Bob Dalton, or Grat neither. Emmitt was okay. Emmitt wasn't too bad, he told himself. He knew there'd be others with Bob. Bob always wanted to go in with plenty of guns blazing.

"I ought to just turn around and go on back to my sweet, loving wife," he told the horse. But the horse gave no advice, no opinion if he should or shouldn't.

"If I wasn't already practically there, I would," he said to the air with its autumn crispness. Small gusts of wind swept up along the road, bestirred the fallen leaves, caused them to do a tired jig like the risen dead, then rest again.

It was the dying season, autumn was, his daddy always said. Like an old man who's taken to his bed and awaits the death that will come when the snow begins to fall. Bears take to their den and everything that don't die holes up, his daddy said. Winter is the dreadful news delivered by an unwanted messenger, like a late-night knock at the door.

He wondered what Edith was doing just that moment. Perhaps bathing in the copper tub, her long dark curls wet and heavy as kelp against her small round head, the water sluicing from her slender bare limbs, glistening over her small firm breasts. Again he was bestirred by the thought of her and whispered in near agony of wanting, "God damn."

CHAPTER 2

The count was six men now that he had arrived, and six horses, encamped in the timber of old man Adams's farm. They'd camped down the hill along Onion creek. He didn't know why it was called that, none of them did. It smelled like mud and dead fish, not onions.

Just at dusk they had stopped at the farmer's house and it was Bob, featuring himself a negotiator, who did the talking.

The old man had come and stood in the doorway, a Sears Roebuck shotgun in his hands. His white hair stood up like a pullet's feathers. There in the shadow behind him stood the woman. The light within the cabin a greasy yellow.

"We'd like to camp for the night," Bob said. "If it's all right with you."

Adams squinted, saw they were heavily armed, each man bearing three or four handguns about his person, plus the butts of Winchesters sticking from their saddlesocks.

"Well, I reckon you could," he said sheepishly, feeling his wife's boney fingers poking him in the back.

"Thankee kindly," Bob said. "We won't be no trouble to you. Be gone from here first light. It'll be like we never existed."

He wanted to ask where they were headed with all that hardware strapped to their persons, but thought better of it. He knew them but he did not let on. Just nodded and said, "Stay long as you care to."

But they'd already turned their horses about and were walking them down toward the stand of timber, the sound of the creek so faint it hardly qualified as a whisper in the growing darkness.

They unsaddled their mounts, aiming to use the saddles to rest their heads upon, and unrolled their soogins for beds. Grat gathered some broken pieces of limbs and started a fire with a Blue Diamond match from a box he carried in his saddlepockets. Emmitt broke out the coffee pot and a bag of Arbuckle. Powers went to relieve his bladder, the sound of the creek running giving him the urge. Ever since that chippy in Tahlequah it seemed he had to piss every five minutes, and it burned like hell. Broadwell sat upon the ground and pulled his boots off his aching feet. They were half a size too small and pinched what he called his "dogs." Broadwell was vain about the size of his feet.

"My dogs is barking like hounds got a coon trapped up in a tree," he said, massaging them through his worn socks.

Bob sort of surveyed the lay of things, squatted by the fire, his palms catching some of the fire's meager heat. The flames reflected in his gray eyes.

Bill Doolin cared for the equines, strapping feedbags on and running his hands over their sweated backs before coming and squatting across from Bob, the flickering fire between them casting their features in shadow and light. The light reached up in the limbs of hardwoods and flickered as if a séance was about to begin.

Up in the house the old man stood by a darkened window looking down toward the timber. The old man's woman stood next to him.

"What they doin,' Ad?" she whispered.

"They built 'em a fire is all I know."

"A fire! Lord, I hope they don't set the whole woods to burn down."

She leaned in closer, saw what the farmer saw—what looked like fireflies in among the timber, only they weren't fireflies at all, but sparks that threatened if one took hold of those bare late-autumn trees the entire wood would go. Praise Jesus it had most recently rained and the timber wasn't so dry as it could have been.

"How come them to stop by here in the first place?" she said into his good ear. "Of all the country to stop in, they had to pick here?"

"How am I supposed to know the answer to that?" he said, without taking his gaze from the watery window glass.

His clothing smelled of tobacco and woodsmoke and old sweat from days'-long usage without benefit of a change or a bath. It was the scent of him she'd come to be familiar with over thirty-odd years. She made him bathe once a month in the creek whether he liked it or not except in the coldest of winter, and she bathed there too, although this time of year the water was getting mighty chill.

"How come?" she said it again when he did not reply the first time.

"I reckon 'cause I know some of 'em and they know me," he said.

"You know them boys, some of 'em?" she repeated.

"Knew their daddy a long times back. Knew that oldest boy was a marshal that got himself killed. But these particular boys? Nah, not too overly much. Just Bob, a little, know *of* 'em is all."

"They're trouble, Ad. You see how they was armed? You ought to go down and run 'em off."

"Why, woman, you must be crazy," he said with growing irritation at her questions. "Whyn't you go on up to bed and let things be?"

"I had a premonition. Before they come I had one, Ad. It portended trouble, black death it were."

He scoffed at her musings and superstitions, clucked his tongue, and said, "They'll be lit out in the morning."

"They might come kill us in our beds," she said, her voice wavering. "How do you know they won't? And rape me too."

"Why'd they want to kill us for?" he said, still looking down there toward the timber, the winking light, then up at the sickle of a moon, what folks referred to as an "Indian hunting moon." It seemed to teeter just atop the timber, like you could toss a rope around one horn and drag it to the earth and watch it buck, a furious thing. He did not comment on her expressed fear of being raped because it was too ridiculous, he deemed. She'd stopped laying with him years back but for when he would not take her refusal, and then she allowed it only grudgingly. She'd told him once he ought to put away such notions, his age.

"You reckon I should take 'em some biscuits, Ad? Maybe do a little jig for 'em, seeing's how we're being real friendly to 'em and all?"

"You go do what you want," he said. "I'm going to bed."

"I don't feature letting 'em stay on the property."

"Then best you tell 'em that when you run them biscuits down and do your little dance performance for 'em."

She followed him on up to the loft bedroom, like one shadow following another, quiet, the way they'd done it for all those years—irritated, impatient, unsettled with each other. She feared he'd want to rut with her and he feared she wouldn't.

The boys squatted on their bootheels around the fire, all but for Doolin who stood apart now, one hand bracing him against the rough trunk of a black walnut tree. He'd begun to doubt the plan Bob had set forth.

Bob, there in the circle of light, pontificating on the plan itself: bold and boastful, bordering on braggadocio, as was his wont whenever the subject of Frank and Jesse James and the Younger gang entered Bob's jealous thoughts to the point of spilling off his tongue.

He drew a hasty map in the dirt that nobody could see, really, as he explained it for the umpteenth time: how they were going to rob both banks in Coffeyville at the same time.

"This here's the plaza," he said, tapping a crude triangle scraped in the dirt.

Coffeyville, which was just at that hour asleep ten or so miles to the north of them and across the borderline, was quiet and peaceful as a mother's dreams of her child. A town of honest hardworking folks, except for an occasional miscreant or two who might be locked up in the town jail for disorderly conduct or public drunkenness. It was a town that lacked scandal and liquor and most certainly gunplay.

Coffeyville, a place of churches and well-kept homes, of businesses and honest men, tried and true. A town that prospered more on hope than reality, clean as a preacher's shirt it was.

Coffeyville, just a sleepy little burg that was about to learn what hell in the breech meant, that no matter how safe and decent a town was, it only took evil to put asunder such notions and strike as sudden as a summer storm.

Bob, Grat, and Emmitt Dalton knew Coffeyville, Kansas, as easily as they knew their own skin. They'd grown up near the town. The crude dirt map was for the benefit of Bill Powers or, as he sometimes called himself, Tom Evans, and for the benefit of Dick Broadwell, also a man with several aliases that included Tom Moore and Texas Jack. Neither had stepped foot in Coffeyville before. Though Bill Doolin had, was arrested there once over a beer squabble, a youthful prank.

As Bob talked, Broadwell brooded. Some who knew him, knew of his late history, took to calling him Poor Richard for the indignity he'd most recent suffered when his scheming young wife disappeared with every last cent. Such calumny had left him brokenhearted and disillusioned about humans in general and women in particular.

So Bob explained it to Broadwell and Bill Powers—or whatever he chose to call himself that night—how the banks were right across a plaza from each other, how brother Grat and Dick and Bill would slip into the Condon Bank while himself and brother Emmitt and—he looked over his shoulder at Doolin—Bill Doolin would take down the First National.

"Shit, they won't know what hit them," Bob concluded. "We'll show 'em our pistol barrels and take the money while they're trying to hold their water. Simple as that. In and out in five minutes. Not even the fuckin' James boys ever pulled off something like it—robbing two banks at the same time."

Emmitt took a rag and used it to hold the handle of the coffee pot and filled their cups with black-as-tar Arbuckle that had the grit of coffee grounds in the bottom that would worry your teeth.

Broadwell said, "Thankee, sweety," when Emmitt filled his cup.

Emmitt was the youngest of them, a handsome, almost feminine-faced youth.

He came over to Doolin to fill his cup, but Doolin waved him off.

"Makes me have to get up in the middle of the night and piss," Doolin said.

Somewhere hidden in the timber a barn owl hooted softly—two, three, four times—then fell silent.

"This is our last job, boys," Bob said, blowing steam from his cup, holding it delicately with both gloved hands. "We'll have us enough money to go to South America and get away from these goddamn laws. Heck Thomas and them."

Grat seemed to sulk, as was his usual demeanor that grew worse when he drank, which more and more had become his common state of being. Of all three Dalton brothers encamped, Grat was the most dangerous in Doolin's estimation. Grat had a dull brain and acted and reacted without a lot of thought being put into it. He had no talent for planning. You hit him, he hit you twice as hard. Bob told him to jump, Grat didn't even ask what for, he just jumped. Same with a gun. Doolin knew that if anyone got killed tomorrow, it would probably be Grat who killed them.

Dick Powers told a joke about a traveling salesman and a farmer's daughter. They laughed and Emmitt said, "Tell another."

"What say ye?" Bob asked, half turning to stare at Doolin who hadn't so much as moved an inch and still leaned against the walnut.

"About what?"

"About my plan to rob them Coffeyville banks?"

"I think you're signing you all's death warrant."

Bob blanched at the comment. The two of them always had an uneasy and tenuous relationship since the get go, since Emmitt introduced them. Emmitt was a good egg in Bill's mind, a boy out for adventure, it seemed, more than anything. Like most boys his age.

"You got a better plan, let's hear it," Bob said, his voice with an edge sharp as a stropped razor.

"I do, but this ain't it."

"What is it?" Grat chimed in, his voice a threat, like the low growl of a cur dog.

"You all do what you want," Bill said coolly. "Don't let me stop you."

Emmitt did his best to mediate by saying, "I heard this joke about a dote whose pap sent him to town to sell a hog . . ."

Then he proceeded to tell it and Powers and Broadwell laughed and Grat said, "Shit, Em, only thing funny about you is your teeny tallywacker." Then they all laughed, including Bob. All but Bill Doolin.

Doolin had made up his mind about the Coffeyville run because of a dream he had the night before, a dream in which he saw bloody corpses—his own included—laid out like shot coyotes upon a board sidewalk.

Doolin was a believer in dreams and mindful of spiritual matters. His mother had the ability to speak directly to the dead and had passed some of her spiritual gifts on to him. It wasn't like he could see the future and predict what was to happen, but more an ominous sense that came over him when something bad was going to happen, and then it did. But the night before, he actually saw the bodies so vividly it started him from his sleep.

He'd sat bolt upright and listened and looked about. But he heard only the wind rustling through the last of the autumn leaves that still clung to the trees, and saw only the blackest night. And in the seeing and listening to his ominous surroundings, he felt dread—the sort of dread that gnawed at a man's vitals like some unseen beast.

Of the dead in his dreams, only his own face did he recognize.

But it was plain enough they were riding into their own destruction.

All that day he hoped maybe it was just the jitters, that being a new husband with a new wife had made him a might overly cautious.

But no, here encamped in the farmer's woods, the sense of dread was even worse. The way the shadows jumped and danced against the black trunks of trees and over their faces and glittered in their eyes and sometimes appeared black as depthless holes. Then there was the pattern of coffee grounds in the bottom of his cup, a foretelling of death the way he read them.

That night, wrapped in his blanket, he could not sleep and lay awake until the first light appeared cold and gray.

Bob was the second out of his blankets and rousted the others from their sleep and listened to them grumble with heads heavy with whiskey-laced coffee from the night before. They shivered and tugged on their boots and stood and stamped their feet down into them and tucked in their shirttails, then went off into the bushes to do their business.

Again it was Emmitt who set about making the morning coffee, having gathered loose wood for the fire.

Up in the house, the old man gazed toward the timber and saw a thread of smoke rising above the trees. The ground fog was too heavy to see much except here and again the movement of a ghostly figure.

The woman lay in her bedclothes yet. Surely as she had expected the arrival of strangers had set the old man off the night before, stirred in him passion that long should have died out and he had rutted with her and now the rutting had left her partially disoriented and feeling a bit mean. She hated even the hint of such doings at her age. Figured the thing that set him off last night had to do with him being scared of those fellows, maybe fearful they would kill him and her and he'd never get no more chances at her. Least that's how she reasoned it. Still, she hadn't cared for it and hoped privately he wouldn't do it again for months, if ever.

"They still down there?" she said.

"Yes," he said and did not remark on the previous night's doings, for it no longer mattered now that it was over.

"How long you reckon they're stayin'?"

"Said they'd be gone first light," he said and strapped his galluses over his bony shoulders. Then he turned and looked at her and saw barely that which was left of her former comeliness and tried hard to remember the days of their sparking and how it had been that they couldn't keep their hands off each other, but anymore it was a lot like living with an aunty, say.

"Maybe you could fix up some breakfast," he said and went on down the ladder to stir a fire in the iron stove.

They moved about in silence, the fog clinging to their legs like gray rags. Drank their Arbuckle and chewed strips of beef jerky in silence except for the grinding of teeth, each man gathering himself enough to carry out the day's order of business. The crude map Bob had scratched in the dirt the night before remained as he had scratched it. So too the stick he'd scratched it with.

"Don't believe I'll ride on into Coffeyville with you boys," Doolin stated flatly as he stood across from Bob and the others saddling their mounts.

"Why the hell not?" Bob said.

"I think it's a damn fool idea, what you propose," Bill said, smoothing the horse blanket over the back of his bloodbay. "Those rubes in Coffeyville will spot you boys inside of a minute."

Bob snorted, said, "Hell, you don't think I counted on it? We got false beards." And he pulled one out from his saddlepockets and held it to his face.

Doolin, restraining an outright laugh, said, "Shit, Bob, I reckon you figured on every angle. Ain't nobody gonna recognize you boys with such fine disguisement."

"Then why the hell'd you come for?" Bob's face turned red as a country beet, such was his anger.

"Same as the rest of you boys. Needed the money."

"And now of a sudden you decided you don't?"

"I reckon I still do, but it'll be awfully god-damn hard to spend if I'm laid out stiff and dead as a hog at slaughtering time."

"Then you should have said something last night when I asked you."

"I'm saying it now."

Doolin could feel Bob's hard gaze on him, but it was of no consequence. His mind was made up. He could almost feel the bullets punching his gut if he rode into Coffeyville with these dolts.

"Well it was you I was counting on to go with Emmitt and me into the First National while the other three slipped into the Condon. Now it throws off our numbers."

Doolin didn't reply but instead dropped the saddle upon his horse's back, hooking the stirrup up on the horn and reaching under for the belly cinch.

The bloodbay swung its head around and looked at him and stamped a back hoof but did not nicker nor raise a fuss. The rest of the horses on the line stood quietly waiting to be saddled as well.

The first sparkle of sun low through the tree limbs had already begun to burn off the fog and with its burning, revealed the swale of brown grass and ripple of creekwater over stones, and farther up the old man's cabin came into shape, so that the world that surrounded them looked newly made and as though they were seeing it for the first time.

"That cuts it with us, then," Bob growled. "Go on and skin out if that's what you want. We don't need you any damn ways. We'll take those banks and be richer for it." He looked around for approval from the others but got nothing but dull-eyed looks, especially from Grat, perhaps the dullest of the brood. Emmitt averted his elder brother's gaze shyly, like a debutante being asked to dance for the first time.

Doolin looked at them, saw ghosts as he tightened the cinch of his saddle, put a foot in the stirrup, and swung aboard the patient horse.

"There's better jobs we could pull," he said, glancing over at Emmitt. "Better and more practical. But that's up to you all."

Then he turned the gelding's head out toward the road that ran up past the house and away from the timber. He wanted to tell them about his premonition, but what good would it do to talk to a man like Bob Dalton about premonitions? Bob or Grat, either one, both of them former United States deputy marshals, men with temperaments hard as cold steel and stubborn as Missouri mules.

Well, let it be and go on home to Edith, he told himself as he rode past the farmhouse. She needs you more than the ol' grim reaper.

The old man was standing on the porch, a corncob pipe clenched in his teeth, the bowl of it held in one boney claw of a hand. The old woman was there too in a gingham dress and poke bonnet, also puffing on a smoking pipe. They watched him keenly but he went on as if they weren't there, as if he wasn't there either.

The old man called, "You boys leaving?"

Doolin went on without an answer.

Otherwise, it looked to be a pretty day.

Chapter 3

The mustachioed George Newcomb stood in his front yard in his long drawers holding an empty galvanized wash pan he'd just tossed dirty water from, the ground dark with it, when he saw a rider coming.

"Rose," he called to the dugout, "get my six-shot and be quick about it."

The boys called him Bitter Creek Newcomb because an old cowboy song he liked to sing had those words in it. When not being an outlaw, he could be downright enjoyable company, some said. A charmer of women and girls, a backslapper when drinking, a joke teller, and loose-footed as they came.

The girl came to the doorway, waif thin, dressed in naught but a scant sleeping shift that revealed hard little breasts, a mere fourteen years old, and said, "Who is it, George? She had a large Schofield .44-40 caliber revolver in her hand with rosewood grips and a blue steel barrel. It felt to her heavy as brick. George called it his thumb-buster.

"Bring it to me," he said and she did.

"Can't tell yet," he said. "But it could likely be the laws."

"I only see one," she said. "Would they send just one?"

"Hell, I'm supposed to know what they'd send?" he said roughly, taking the Schofield from her hand and breaking it open to check the loads then snapping it shut again. She didn't like him much when he was in a foul mood and stood behind him slightly in case it came to a shooting. He was bare-chested and in just his trousers, his galluses hanging down, his bare feet dusty.

"You best go on get inside and take up the Winchester, like I showed you," he ordered.

"But I want to be with you . . ."

"Jesus, but if you wasn't such a sweet little thing . . ." He could not stay angry with her.

He thumbed back the hammer of the revolver, holding it down along his leg ready to go. No use to try and run. Too late for that. It was just the one fellow is all he could see and he could handle just one, he figured.

But he didn't have to. It was Doolin.

They could have been brothers in looks, both handsome and dark featured, but for Doolin being as emaciated-appearing as he was and George being a man of considerable heft and size.

"It's Doolin," he said to the girl. "Go fix us some coffee, splash some sour mash in it too, and fry up some scrapple. I know he'll damn well be hungry. Man's as skinny as a wormy dog."

She scatted back to the dugout as Bill Doolin rode up, his horse lathered with sweat. He dismounted, dropped the reins, and the horse walked over to the watering tank Newcomb had fashioned from an old cast-iron bathtub he'd dragged out of a burned-out hotel in Enid.

Doolin glanced at the piece Bitter Creek was holding.

"You aiming to kill me, George?"

"Someone, maybe, but not you," George said with a toothy smile that looked like he had a mouthful of piano keys. "I see you come alone?"

"Wait until I tell you," Doolin said.

"What?"

They meandered over to the dugout and then squatted in the dust where the shade was best and upwind from the privy while the girl brought them each a cup of liquor-laced coffee with a splat of condensed milk in it like Newcomb favored and squatted down next to her bearded lover. Bill gave her a look, a sinful but doe-eyed young thing what could make a man think twice about being faithful to a wife back home.

"Don't worry, got some scrapple frying and biscuits in the oven warmer. Be ready soon enough. How you be, Bill?"

Doolin and others often teased George for being a cradle robber soon as he'd taken up with Rose Dunn, young as she was. Her brood of brothers didn't necessarily care for her taking up with a man old as George was. But at least her care and feeding was off their hands. The brothers were by trade butchers, and bounty hunters when not running their butcher shop. But the butcher business did not pay enough alone to keep them in up to their hocks in whores and whiskey.

"Doing just fine, little sister, what about you all?"

She glanced at George, said, "Oh, we're still in love, if that's what you're asking."

Bitter Creek grunted like an old married man, said, "Most of the time, anyways."

They sipped some of the black lacquer and Bitter Creek made a face and said, "God damn! How much of that popskull'd you put in this?"

Rose gave him an offended look then stood and went back inside the dugout.

"So what is it you have to tell me?" George said.

"Bob Dalton and them got wiped out two days ago in Coffeyville trying to rob the banks there."

"Banks?"

"Yep. It was Bob's idea to rob them both the same time." Doolin set his cup in the dust, wiped his hands on his knees, and reached for his tobacco makings, cigarette papers and Bull Durham pouch.

"It didn't work out so well," he added. "Funny thing is, I had a dream about it and it's what kept me from going along. Else," he said, "I'd be as dead as them."

"The laws got 'em?" George asked. "Heck Thomas and his bunch?"

"No, nothing as glorious as that."

Doolin made a trough in the cigarette paper and tapped in some tobacco, then tightened the drawstring on his pouch with his teeth and tucked it back in his shirt pocket one-handed as he held the as-yet-unfinished cigarette with the other. Then he rolled the paper over and licked the edge and twisted off the ends. He held it for a moment examining his handiwork, then struck a match off his spur rowel and lit the end and took in a lungful of smoke before exhaling it again.

"It was townsfolks," Doolin said. "Shot them boys to rags. Ducks in a shooting gallery." He shook his head, still disbelieving how the Daltons ended up dead in the dirt after all their forays into criminality.

"Who all was with 'em?" Bitter Creek asked, blowing steam off his cup, thinking as he did, *That gal would burn water if given the chance, and her biscuits a schoolboy could use in his slingshot for busting out windows.*

"There was Bob, of course, his brothers Grat and Emmitt, Bill Powers, and poor old Dick Broadwell," Doolin said.

"Jesus . . . they got Broadwell too?"

"I bet they wished they'd had Jesus with them," Doolin said. "Killed four townsmen as well and wounded a couple others. Regular damn old shootout is what it was."

"All dead?"

"All but Emmitt. I read they believe that he *will* die from his wounds. Said he took a full load of buckshot."

"Jesus," Bitter Creek said again. "They're gone kill us all before it's all said and done, ain't they, Bill?"

"I reckon. Between the laws and itchy-finger citizens we'll be put under the sod sooner or later. We're not well loved in this country. Not like Jesse and them were in theirs."

"Well, hell, Jesse got shot by his own kin," George offered.

"Yes, but not the common folks in Missouri. They thought that devil was Robin Hood or some such."

Rose Dunn brought out two plates of beans and scrapple and her hard-as-soapstone biscuits.

"You best eat you some of this, Bill," she said. "You could use some meat on your bones." Bitter Creek didn't care for the way she said it: flirty like.

"Thankee kindly, Rose. Smells delicious."

"What's this I heard you say about the Daltons?" she asked.

"They got slaughtered the other day over in Kansas."

She remained silent for a while, then: "Even that pretty Emmitt?"

"Not total graveyard dead yet, but soon, they're saying—the newspapers is."

"He was a right pert boy," she said. "And kindly too."

Doolin could make out just about all of her under that thin shift with the sun showing through from behind her. He didn't know how George stood it, bedding such a nubile young child as she without his heart giving way. But stood it he surely had, for he looked fat and sassy as a well-fed coon.

"We gone do something soon?" George said, looking over at him as he spooned beans into his mouth, the grease glistening in his moustaches.

"I reckon we better while we still can. Bob and them was planning on using the money to head to Argentina, get out of the country. Said it was getting hotter around here than a two-dollar pistol."

"He'd be damn right about that," George said, wiping his mouth with the back of his wrist.

"Well, we ought to do something," Bill said washing down the last of what he ate with more of the coffee. "Mighty fine meal, Rose."

"We ought to," Bitter Creek said.

"I'd favor some pretty clothes," Rose said.

"You look swell in that," Bill said, nodding toward her. What she had on not leaving much to the imagination.

George looked on broodingly, and anxious to get on the owlhoot trail again. A man could only take just so much domesticity, even if it was with such a sweet flower as she.

Bill smoked. George finished eating. Rose Dunn—the Rose of Cimarron some had taken to calling her—looked on.

"I might have a few ideas in mind," Doolin said. "Whyn't you come round my place in a week or two?"

"You don't want to do nothing right now?"

"I do, for sure. But before I do anything, I need to take care of some homework," he said with a wink, the lovely Rose in her near altogether rousing desire that had already been floating near the surface in him. He needed some time with Edith.

Chapter 4

I knew all those boys—Bob, Grat, Emmitt, all of 'em. They were good boys once. Lawmen, some of them at one time. Good honest types. You take Frank, for instance. Got himself killed over in the Cherokee Nation while trying to arrest some horse-thieving whiskey runners. Took one through the chest and, the way I heard it, begged for his life but they shot him square in the face while he lay upon the ground. He wan't but twenty-nine years old and sure as hell did not deserve to die so ingloriously. But then what lawman ever does, and yet they do.

Don't know but it was the killing of their older brother that drove the rest of 'em to the dark side—that, and greed of the easy dollar. Why work in a bank when you can rob it, I guess they thought like. I reckon we're all of us cut from a different cloth, and what turns one man bad and another good is something I reckon only the Lord God in heaven knows for sure.

I do know this: it was hard seeing those boys in death, so young as they were there in Coffeyville, trussed up with baling wire so they could be posed for photographs.

Bad as I wanted to catch 'em, I would have much preferred capturing them alive and seeing they got due justice under the law, because more than anything else in this old world, I believe in the law and that it must remain supreme over all else or we got nothing but chaos and might just as well everyone arm themselves and kill whoever they hold a grudge against. Some do anyway. Kill or be killed, that's what the law of the land would become without true justice as upheld by the courts and the bona fide lawmen.

The bodies were stiff and sad-faced in death. Grat, maybe the toughest of the bunch that day, looked peaceful as a child. Like he'd just laid down and took a nap 'neath a willow tree. And Bob, well, Bob looked surprised as hell. I guess death overtook him when he wasn't quite expecting it. Knowing him, he probably believed there wasn't no bullet ever had his name on it. Bill Powers looked like he was just plain peaceful. And Dick Broadwell had a slight smile, as though he was almost glad it had finally ended—riding the owlhoot trail, being hounded and always on the run. I can see how a fella wanted by the laws might feel that way after a while. Give me liberty or give me death.

I went on up to the jail to the second floor where they were keeping a death watch on Emmitt. He was pale as a ghost and in much discomfort. First words he said to me were: "You always was a day late and a dollar short, Heck. But I reckon you caught us at last . . ." Coughed blood into an already bloody handkerchief balled in his fist. "They peppered me good, Heck, only wished they'd finished the job."

I truly felt sorry for the boy. He'd fallen in with a bad lot led by his older brothers. I asked him some of the details. He was mighty emotional at first, saying how they'd hauled his dead brothers Bob and Grat up to the room and had him identify their corpses. Same with Bill Powers, whom he referred to as Tom Evans, and Dick Broadwell, who he called Jake Moore, their aliases. Tears wetted his cheeks.

Then when he gathered himself some, he told me and the others in the room how he and Bob were coming out of the front door of the First National Bank, and soon as they did the bullets were flying and Bob stepped into the street and fired off his Winchester, cussing like a teamster as he did.

"We ran back inside the bank and went out the back door into the alley and ran into some fellow with a six-shooter who Bob killed straightaway. Then we hightailed it to the back of Wells Brothers to

get our horses where we had them tied in the alley at a wooden fence. Bob kept up a withering fire to keep the others off us. I mostly just prayed we'd get out of there alive."

He paused and asked for some water and somebody gave it to him and he drank it with a painful expression on his face.

"I didn't see Cubine," he said, referring to George Cubine, a citizen of that town who became a victim of the gun fury. "But anyways, Bob was shot down just about the time we reached our horses and could not get aboard his. I could have got away, but saw Bob fall and rode back to him. He held out his hand and I was endeavoring to pull him up behind me when I was disabled."

Again he paused and lay back, as weary as a man who'd worked all day in the hot sun. With eyes closed, he whispered hoarsely, "I wish they'd have finished me too, Heck, I truly do." It was the second time he said that and I believe he was serious—that he'd rather be dead than the way he was.

Sheriff Callahan then told me it was the barber, Seamen, who cut Emmitt down with a double-barrel blast from his shotgun.

"Wonder that boy is still breathing Coffeyville air," the lawman said. "How many you know, Heck, that's taken a full load of buckshot at close range and lived to tell about it?"

"Well, you all wiped out a mess of 'em," I said. Too bad you didn't get them all. There's still some of 'em, running loose."

"We got all we wanted," he said. "I don't reckon we'll see the likes of 'em again soon."

"I wouldn't be so sure of that," I told him. "Those Daltons are harder to lick than a room full of wildcats."

I went back out again into the peaceful streets where some business owners were already washing away the blood with buckets of soapy water, and others stood counting and commenting on the bullet holes in the Condon's handsome plate glass windows and the chips in the plaster.

The mood over the town was the same as after a day when a

cyclone had come through it. Eight dead, a number of wounded. Such a pretty day it was too. I knew then I'd have to catch the rest of that bunch—what some of the newspapers had started calling the Oklahombres. Men such as Bill Doolin, George Bitter Creek Newcomb, Charlie Pierce, Tulsa Jack Blake, Dynamite Dick Clifton, Arkansas Tom, Ol Yantis, and plenty others. I had to clean up that mess—me and Chris Madsen and Bill Tilghman. Some of the newspapers had tagged us with the moniker "The Three Guardsmen"—something we were proud to be known by.

We relied on each other, but also went our separate ways, spreading out over the Indian Nations like the plague to capture or kill the others. Trouble was, those fellas were as tough as any of us, as fearless too, and more than a few of us were likely to end up as dead as the Daltons in Coffeyville.

Chapter 5

Bill Doolin rose from his and Edith's midnight bed, a silver blade of moonlight knifed into the room and cut in two the quilted coverlet. He walked to the lone window and looked out into the monochrome night, a photograph with too little flash.

"What is it?" his young wife said.

He cannot define her there in the room's darkness, even with the moonlight, but he long ago committed her looks to memory and could see her as plain as day even if he were blind: her fresh pert face and dark ringlets of hair framing her head, the slight curve of her belly, the hauteur of her firm small breasts, the silky dark triangle of her sex.

He often teases her about how such a charming and civilized young lady could take up with a wild old dog such as he. To which she always smiled that mysterious smile and said, "Darling Bill, how could any girl resist such a handsome rogue? Don't you know that opposites attract?"

It arouses him every time.

"What do you see out there?" she asked.

"Nothing," he replied, looking out into the phosphorous yard, the world and everything in it the color of unpolished silver. In a far room at the other end of the house slept her father, a preacher man of the first rank: a circuit-riding Presbyterian who went about trying to save the world with mule and Bible, one cabin at a time. White, red, Negro, it made no difference to him. A saved soul was a saved soul. He was a soft-spoken man who did not entirely approve of his daughter's choice in marriage. There was no one thing he could put his finger on when it came to Doolin and he was therefore wont to voice loudly his objection, fearing she would simply elope with the man, for he has seen the way she was around him. Better that he bless the union than to curse it.

"Come back to bed," she said. "I'm cold."

He was reluctant to abandon the window, sensing somebody was out there watching the house. He kept one pistol under his pillow and another beneath the bed. He knew that time was a precious thing, that it would not last. The stories he'd read in the newspapers about the Coffeyville raid were lurid and remindful that the number of minutes, hours, days, weeks were running out for him, unless he could score big and clear out of the country. United States Deputy Marshal Heck Thomas was a bloodhound on a scent, and so too the others—that Dane, Chris Madsen, and the steely-eyed Bill Tilghman. All of them legal killers sanctioned by the government, as far as he was concerned. *They do it for the money same as me,* he thought.

Without turning from the window, he said, "We might be gone have to move away soon."

She surely knew of his activities. Maybe not all the lurid details, but she had to know the money he came home with just didn't drop out of the sky. He felt no need to trouble her with any of it. Just told her he was partners in the livestock trade, buying and selling cattle and horses. She did not question more than what he had to say.

"I'm a man who does manly things to provide for me and my own," he told her early on. "You must be content with letting me do what I must to provide for you and your father and be of good cheer."

He saw the worry in her eyes. She was not an uneducated or silly woman. But her love for him blinded her to all else and so she'd let it be—the questions about his comings and goings. Still, there were newspapers. But whatever she knew, or her papa knew, had never become a subject of conversation between them all.

She remained silent there in the bed and slowly he turned and climbed under the covers and pulled her to him. He felt the warmth of her breath against his neck. His hand glided over her hip and came to rest between her legs.

"When?" she said. "About the move?"

He shrugged.

"Can't say rightly. Me and Bitter Creek and some of the boys are aiming to go buy some cattle and sell them up in the Nations tomorrow. I'll know more when I get back."

Again the silence, the steady breathing, the rise and fall of her chest as she curled her back against him.

"Damn, woman, but you do glitterfy my blood."

"Good," is all she said.

Something flies in the night, something with heavy thudding wings, its shadow crosses the moon—an owl no doubt, or perhaps a thing a witch might conjure.

Her father laid awake listening to what, he didn't know. The voice of God perhaps, whispering to him in a faint confused language. He feared for his daughter that the man lying with her will someday bring her heartbreak. He has known such men before—was one himself, once. He prayed in silence, his pale thin lips moving dryly.

"Dear Lord, if it be thy will . . ."

Chapter 6

They rode two by two with one driving the wagon. You could tell by the way it lay heavy on its springs there was a hell of a load in the bed there under the green tarp.

Four slaughtered beeves, butchered out, hides stripped off so that no brand could have been found even by a lawman who might be looking for one.

The wagoner halted in front of the butcher shop in Pawnee, Oklahoma Territory, and hauled back on the reins, set the foot brake, and wrapped the reins around it twice before climbing down.

The outriders tied off at the hitch rail and dismounted.

The wagon's driver unlocked the front door of the butcher shop, then said, "Bring in them beeves."

The four brothers—Bee, Calvin, Dal, and George Dunn—obeyed their eldest brother Bill, though they didn't like it much, having to do the heavy lifting, but did it anyway and hustled the butchered animals inside, past the glass case, and to the back room and hung the carcasses on hooks near a wide butcher block table with a set of sharp knives and a couple of cleavers laid out. The sawdust floor was congealed in spots by old blood.

The carried carcasses had stained the shoulders of the brothers' coats with blood as well by time they'd finished their labor.

Bill Dunn was pleased with the haul. Stolen beef, butchered and sold as steaks and roasts, was, but for the cost of labor, a one hundred percent profit business. Unless you got caught.

Bill did not intend on any of them getting caught.

By the time Sheriff Canton sauntered in, the brothers had taken up residence in chairs, two inside and two out, with Bill Dunn behind the glass case wrapping and packaging a few steaks for a cookout later at the ranch he shared with his brothers and sister, Rose, and of course that paramour of hers, Bitter Creek Newcomb.

"You boys look bloody," the lawman said with a hint of accusation. "Been on a meat-buying expedition?"

"That's right," Bill replied. "Got a good price on a roast this week: fifty cents a pound. Call it the lawdog special, just for you."

There was always a tension between the brothers and anyone who wore a badge, a tension as taut as freshly strung barbed wire and just as prickly too.

"Got a bill of sale for what I saw you boys haul in?"

"Sure, got one right here," Bill said, producing the phony document with the name of the seller as Charley Three Dog, Cherokee Nation.

Canton took his time looking it over. Couldn't prove anything one way or the other, so he handed it back.

"See you butchers around," he said and walked out, past the two sitting outside on chairs tipped back on their rear legs—Calvin and Bee. Bee had the stare of a killer. So did the others, but Bee could stare death right into you, Canton thought.

"Them boys is bad news that I'm going to write the final sentence to," he told himself as he walked back up the street. "They think they're sly as foxes, but they ain't. They got blood on more than just their clothes, I'd bet. Got blood down in their souls, murderous blood, and it wasn't just beeves they killed."

A little chill trickled down his backbone. Old mama Dunn had sure raised herself a brood of vipers.

"What you think he wanted?" Dal said inside the shop.

"Same as always, hoping to catch us at something, but he never will," Bill said, finishing his wrapping of the meat in butcher paper and tying it with a length of string he unraveled from a spindle.

"We'll eat good tonight. Have Rose and Bitter Creek up too."

"If we can ever get them out of the blankets," Dal said sourly. He was never for her hitching up with Newcomb, thought Newcomb was way too old for her, thought the outlaw had cast a spell over his little sister, that maybe he was some sort of evil thing walking around in human form. But the other brothers were not so inclined to feel harshly toward the outlaw, mostly because of his good nature, and slightly because of how dangerous of a man he was.

"You ought to let sleeping dogs lie," George joked.

"That ain't a bit funny," Dal said, spitting between his boots planted on the sawdust floor of wide worn planks.

Holly Parrot, the widow of Big Jim Parrot, came in, the little bell above the door tinkling, and all three looked up. She wasn't one of those old dried-up widows either, but fresh-faced and pretty with her hair as red as an autumn maple leaf and a spatter of freckles across a dainty nose and cheekbones. She had pale green eyes to add to her allure. She was much sought after by town bachelors and the married fellows too. And she much enjoyed the game of flirtation with any man bold enough to play it.

"Hello, Bill," she said and greeted the other two in a like manner. George and Dal nearly swooned right out of their chairs when she mentioned them by name. My God in heaven, they thought. What I wouldn't give . . .

She asked Bill if he would pick her out a nice roast and he hopped to saying he'd just gotten in a fresh beef and he'd go in back and cut her one. While she awaited his return she engaged the other two in light conversation, asking them how they'd been and had they yet gone to the opera house to see the new stage show *Hamlet,* performed by a traveling troupe of actors. No, they hadn't, but they were mighty looking forward to it. And so it went for the few minutes it took Bill to return with a nice fat roast.

"Well, there you are, Miz Parrot," Bill said, having wrapped and tied the roast.

"How much do I owe you, Mr. Dunn?"

"One dollar and twenty cents," he said, "but don't tell anyone, it's a special price just for you."

"Oh my," she said breathily, as an actress might—not that Bill or the other Dunn boys knew much about actresses. "You're such a sweet, considerate man."

Bill's cheeks turned rosy and warm.

"Well, I do what I can, and if there's anything else you might be requiring . . ."

It was sort of a double entendre, the way he said it, and they both knew it too and so did George and Dal. They weren't nitwits, after all, and slyly jabbed each other with their elbows behind her back.

"Well, I'll be back tomorrow," she said, and they watched her go and Bill took a kerchief out of his back pocket and wiped the sweat from his forehead.

"Little warm for you, brother Bill?" Dal said, grinning.

"If you louts hadn't been lazing about I might have got somewheres with her," Bill said.

"Shit, brother," George said. "You couldn't get nowheres with a two-dollar whore if you had five dollars in every pocket."

Dal laughed and so did George. Bee and Calvin came in from outside, Bee saying, "Now there goes one fine-looking woman. Maybe I'll set my hat for her."

Calvin was more interested in other things.

"I think I'll walk down to the post office and see what rewards are posted."

"You do that," Bill said. "But only look for the ones with the most money."

They'd most recent gone into the bounty-hunting business, but it was uncertain and unsteady work, even though the payoffs were pretty decent. It required planning and sometimes a dear amount of travel, and that increased expenses, unlike cattle rustling, which was mostly just running the risk of getting caught and getting your head blown off by some stock detective.

Thus far in their newfound endeavor, they'd only killed one man for the bounty money, a whiskey running rapist named Waldo Sanchez. It was Bee who shot him first, but the others pumped some lead into him once he was down and dead just for the sport of it, mostly. They brought him in slung over his horse like a Belgium carpet and dropped him at Sheriff Canton's doorstep who insisted they take him over to Hollister Ogletree's Mortuary before he'd file the paperwork for the $500 reward.

The mortician, upon viewing the body, said, "What were you boys attempting to do to this sucker, turn him into Swiss cheese? You think maybe just three or four bullets would have done the trick?"

They'd spent the money in about two days straight: drinking and whoring. It was the more practical-minded Bill who stated the money sure hadn't lasted long, and the more gregarious Calvin who said, "No, but it sure was good while it *did* last."

"Reckon we ought to go find something to kill besides another Hereford, Dal said. "Yeah, something with two legs and a fat price on they heads."

"I'm all for a drink most current," George said.

They all agreed and emptied the tin cash box and sauntered

up to the nearest saloon and bought themselves a round of drinks.

"You reckon ol' Bitter Creek is putting the horns to our little sister right this instant?" George said as they stood along the bar nursing their drinks. He meant to get Dal's goat.

"Why'd you bring something like that up?" Dal blurted. "That ain't even right, you to say such about our Rose."

Bee shrugged.

"I don't care much for that mustachioed lothario," he said.

"Lissen to him," George said, "using words like lothario."

Bee wiped beer foam from his moustaches with forefinger and thumb and said, "Might be Dal's wishing it was him putting the horns to our sis."

That started a fistfight that lasted ten or so minutes until the big German behind the bar produced a hickory club and threatened to bash in brains, then he bought a round of drinks for the boys, battered and bleeding, and all was peaceful again.

Sheriff Canton, who happened to be sitting off in a corner watching the fireworks, thought, *Jesus, I can't wait to retire and go somewhere less dramatic,* then downed his beer and donned his hat and strolled out into the late afternoon, its reddish light painted across the storefronts and flared in windows like wildfire.

CHAPTER 7

Ol Yantis thought he heard something and sat up in bed suddenly, bolt upright as if he'd been electrocuted. Maybe it had to do with the dream he was having, no doubt brought on by an old newspaper account he'd read on the outhouse wall pasted up there while he did his business the evening before.

The article, yellow and water-stained, spoke of a fellow named Kemler who'd been executed in Buffalo, New York, for killing his wife. Said this Kemler was the first person ever to be executed by means of an electric chair. There was a rendering of the chair. It looked clunky and mortifying. The article went on to say how the electrical generators rigged to the chair sent so much force into the fellow it boiled his brain and smoke rose out of his scalp. Said it "fried" him, as if he'd been thunderstruck. Something about the image of it all had fluttered through the veins of Ol Yantis.

His first cousin Iona, his daddy's sister's girl, lying in the bed next to him, said, "What is it, Ol?"

"Shit if I know," he said, his heart kicking in his chest like the hind legs of a strangled rabbit. His nightshirt was soaked through with sweat.

The first morning light glowed against the window glass soft and gray as cat fur.

"You hear that?" he said.

"What?"

"Thought I heard something."

"What'd you hear?"

"Don't know, damn it to hell, why you have to ask so many questions, woman?"

She cowered at the sound of his voice and half waited for the slap of a hand across her face, something she'd become accustomed to ever since she took up with him. Ol could be a caution when he got scared or worried over something. Theirs was a simple and Spartan existence and had been ever since Iona showed up on his doorstep one day saying she had no place to go, that her ma had passed, her only kin except for Ol. He took her in. The intimacies started shortly thereafter and they'd lived as man and wife now for a few years.

"Git up and fix me something to eat," he ordered.

She rose from the bed without protest and shuffled to the stove in the opposite end of the one large room, their bed shoved up against one wall and a table in between it and the stove on the opposite wall, with a black pipe like a bent arm running out through it.

He pulled on his drawers then socks and stomped his feet down into a pair of rough hide boots before putting on a woolen shirt that he buttoned to the neck. His face was grizzled with unshaven growth of beard and his hair stood up on one side from the pillow. He went to the front door and stood and unbuttoned his front and urinated loudly into the yard, scattering the few chickens who'd come around looking for grubs to peck.

That's when he saw the two riders come out of the red ball of sun that had risen just above the edge of the earth. They looked like a dream he was having.

He could tell by that white horse one of them was Bitter Creek Newcomb. Bitter Creek wouldn't ride nothing but a white horse. The other rode a bloodbay. Had to be Doolin with him. He finished making water and rebuttoned his trouser front.

"Got company," he said into the cabin. "Best put on some

extra grub."

"Who is it?" she said.

"Iona, you ask too many damn questions for a woman."

"I know it," she muttered under her breath.

Seeing the cabin in the distance, Bitter Creek said, "You reckon Ol is still diddling that cousin of his?"

Bill Doolin shrugged, said, "I don't know who else in their right mind would diddle him for no money but a kin."

Bitter Creek grinned, his white teeth flashing in the darkness of his beard like hominy corn in a bin of coal.

Ol stood there in the front door watching them come on, waited until they halted their mounts and unseated themselves.

"Where you boys headed?" he said.

"Here," Doolin said.

"Well, then I reckon you have reached your destination."

"How's that cousin of your'n?" Bitter Creek asked slyly.

"I reckon she's about as fit as that child of your'n," Ol said. "Reckon you boys is hungry?"

"Starved," Bitter Creek said.

"Well, put up them caballos and come on in the house."

As they were unsaddling their horses, Bitter Creek said, "You reckon that's a house?"

"Just barely," Bill said. "I've seen horse sheds better."

They went in and sat at the table and waited as Iona served them coffee and hoecakes and fried fatback.

"You're looking mighty pert," Bitter Creek said.

"Why thankee, George, so are you."

Bitter Creek smoothed his moustaches and beard with the tips of his fingers and then set to eating, pouring some blackstrap molasses over the hoecakes that eventually glistened in his beard.

They ate a while in silence but for their forks scraping the tin plates before Ol said, "I reckon you boys have something in mind to do, the reason you come to get me."

"We do," Bill said. "Might I have some more coffee, Iona?"

"Surely," she said and refilled his cup.

"Thankee," he said.

Bitter Creek eyed her every movement the whole while, even with blackstrap molasses in his beard. He couldn't get over her homeliness.

"Got a little bank over in Spearville in mind," Doolin said.

"That in Kansas?"

Doolin nodded.

"Well," Ol said. "I reckon I could see my way to joining you boys. But let me ask you all something. How close is it that the law is on your heels?"

"They ain't," Doolin said. "Least not anywhere close enough to catch us. They're still counting the dead in Coffeyville."

"So I heard," Ol said. "Iona, whyn't you put something decent on? Everything you own natural is on display."

She went and wrapped a quilt about her and went out then, into the sunstruck yard, to where a covered pail sat by the two wood steps and uncovered it and scooped out some chicken feed and flung it out in the yard and watched the birds come running.

"All god's creatures great and small must eat," she said, then went off to the privy.

"When you boys want to leave for Spearville?" Ol asked.

"Right damn now," Doolin said, standing away from the table.

"No time like the present," Bitter Creek added.

"Sounds good to me. How much you reckon the take will be?"

Doolin shrugged.

"Several thousand, I'd say. Can't be exact. But anything is better than flat pockets like I got now."

"I'm with you on that," Ol said. "Let's burn some daylight, then."

They went out and re-saddled their horses and Ol saddled his, a lineback buckskin that probably had some mustang blood mixed in. It was all muscle and sinew and stood only fifteen hands. Ol being a slight fellow didn't require a big horse.

As they turned to ride off toward Spearville, Ol shouted, "Iona, we'll be back sometime! Keep a light on!"

In the darkness of the privy with its sweet rank odor, Iona closed her eyes and wished for a better world.

Cheswick Bookbinder rubbed the lens of his spectacles clean with his shirttail then readjusted them upon his thorny nose. The bank smelled of wood must, old silver coins and paper money, and Leo Binn's bay rum aftershave. Binn, a young man, a dandy and fop, as far as Cheswick was concerned, stood in the teller's cage next to his own talking to Mr. Warren, who'd come in to deposit some hay money. Cheswick tapped his fingers in anticipation of the next customer who might walk through the bank's double doors.

The sky outside was sullen as was usually the case in November, with a chill wind shivering down the streets of Spearville. Cheswick reminded himself to stop on the way home and buy some Limburger cheese and a can of peaches and two five-cent cigars. Such was the life of a middle-aged bachelor.

Leo finished up with Mr. Warren's account, bid the balding man goodbye, then said, "I think if you don't mind, I'll step out back and smoke a cigarette."

Well, Cheswick *did* mind but he agreed to the plan, thinking as Leo exited the front door that only a fop would smoke a cigarette instead of a cigar and it only proved what Cheswick had thought of him all along. Why Mr. Hammersmith, the bank's owner, had ever hired Leo was beyond him and for the second time that morning he counted the money in his teller's drawer. To think he had to work next to a fop.

He was still counting when the back door burst open. Leo Binn was shoved in front of two men with guns. Two very dangerous-looking men, one of which held the muzzle of his pistol to the back of Leo's skull, while the other rushed to the teller's cage and stuck his gun through the brass bars and shoved a gunny sack through and ordered Cheswick to "Fill 'er up and be damn quick if you value anything about your life!"

The other one ordered Leo to do the same, then when they had finished emptying their drawers into the sack, one ordered Cheswick to open the safe.

"Can't," he said.

"Why can't you, goddamn it?"

"The safe's on a time lock, won't open until nine-thirty."

It was just then ten minutes past nine o'clock.

"Get down on you all's knees," one of them said.

Cheswick could see through the front windows with the gold lettering on them that said in reverse, FIRST NATIONAL BANK, a man sitting on a horse and holding the reins to two other horses.

Then suddenly something hard and painful struck him just above the ear and he fell flat to the floor. As he lay there bleeding, he thought strangely, *I've never been down here before, isn't that funny?*

"Either one of you all gets up sooner than ten minutes and I'll blow out your brains!"

Then the world beneath Cheswick began to tilt and spin.

"Oh . . ." he uttered. "Oh . . ."

There was the sound of scuffling feet, loose coins ringing on the floor—or was that the ring and jingle of spur rowels? The slamming of the door, the thud of hooves quickly fading, then silence but for the buzz of a bottle fly.

"Are you okay, Cheswick?" Leo Binn asked.

After ten hours, the hastily formed posse gave up the chase and turned back. A raging rain had washed out all tracks and signs of the bank robbers.

"They're gone," someone announced, their hats soaked and battered, rain sluicing their brims down their backs and into their eyes.

Bill Doolin and Bitter Creek Newcomb and Ol Yantis returned to Ol's place three days later, Ol handing Iona a package of butcher paper tied with string.

"What is it?" she said.

"Tear it open and see," he said.

She bit the string apart with her surprisingly straight and polished teeth and found in the paper a pretty new gingham dress of light blue, as light blue as a Kansas sky, appropriately purchased with stolen Kansas bank money.

Bill and Newcomb slept in the small barn that evening.

"I'll bet he's right now in there raising hell with her thinking that cheap dress bought him something extra," Newcomb said.

"Please don't mention it," Bill said, "or you're liable to give me nightmares."

Bitter Creek chuckled in the dark, a man of darkly senses of humor.

They were both of them feeling lonely for their own women, Edith and Rose, and wishing they were home with them now doing the same thing they thought maybe Ol was doing with his ugly cousin.

They could see the silver of the moon, some of it, through the holes in the barn's roof where many of the shingles had blown away over time.

It made them even more lonesome.

"We sure didn't make out overly good at that bank job," Newcomb said in the dark. "Not as good as we thought we would."

"Well, at least we didn't get killed none of us," Doolin said. "Didn't get trussed up with wire and have our pictures taken in death holding empty Winchesters like the Daltons and them did in Coffeyville."

"True enough."

"Count your blessings, Newcomb."

"I sure as hell am, including the one of not being inside that cabin with Ol's homely as sin cousin."

"Someday . . ." Doolin said without finishing the thought. "But not this day, anyways."

The light inside the cabin got snuffed out and silence befell the ragged little homestead.

Silence could be a good thing, Bill Doolin thought as he closed his eyes.

CHAPTER 8

It seemed to me like the late autumn of 1892 set off a whole new round of violence, what with the Dalton gang's raid on Coffeyville.

It wasn't but a few weeks later that Bill Doolin put together a gang that robbed the bank in Spearville of an untold amount of money. Leastways nobody was killed in that one.

But the very next day, or perhaps it was two, a posse of deputy marshals trapped Ned Christie at his place in the Rabbit Trap over near Tahlequah and had one hell of a shootout.

Five years previous, me and some of my boys had also run Ned to the ground, and he shot it out with us. And even though I clipped him across the nose with one of my bullets that punched out his eye, he managed to escape.

Ned was just one more miscreant in the Nations, and a bad one too.

It was "Cap" White who stopped by my place and poured forth the details.

"Hell," Cap says as we drank coffee on the front porch of my place and smoked us each a cigar. "I had fifteen deputies with me, tried and true, and we had Ned's place surrounded. You'd a thought he'd had sense enough to give up, but you know that sucker well as I do. He wasn't about to just lay down and surrender."

"I know it," I said. "Remember me and him have tangled before."

"Shot out his eye, didn't you?"

"I did but it didn't slow him down any."

Cap shuddered. "Imagine a fellow with his eyeball gouged out by a shell and still keep running."

"He's more rabbit than a rabbit's a rabbit," I said.

"Well, he had several folks in the house with him, including some women, and we told him to at least let the women go, which he did. Say, I don't reckon you got some bug juice you could spill into this coffee, would you, Heck? I ain't complaining that the coffee's rough or nothing, just that my nerves are still a bit frayed."

I went in the house and come out with a bottle of Old Tub and unscrewed the cap and let him administer what medicine he thought he needed then added just a dollop to my own coffee too. Felt like a cold coming on and figured the medicine might help.

"Well, anyway," Cap continued. "We kept up firing back and forth the whole day, back and forth but to little effect other'n some of us had burn holes in our clothes from Ned and them's bullets passing through our coats and such."

"How'd you flush 'em out?" I asked.

Cap waved a hand still grimed from all the black powder he and the others shot up that day. Waved it like he was swatting gnats out of the air.

"We finally sent for a cannon."

"I bet Ned never reckoned to have a cannon thrown down on him."

Cap shook his head.

"I reckon he didn't. But it didn't do no good. We shot it so hot it blew itself up. I was beginning to think that Indun couldn't be killed, that maybe the Lord himself was a redskin and not white and favored Ned."

"I've been thinking that for over five years," I said. "It's like he's some sort of mythical being."

"Like Jesus," Cap said. "Only red."

"Have to admit, but for that missing eye, and with all that long hair and thin little moustache, he does resemble somewhat the renderings of our Lord and Savior."

"Did," Cap corrected. "He don't no more."

"How'd you close the deal eventually?"

"Got in close enough to lob in some dynamite and it set the place afire. Thought for a time there Ned would just let himself get burned up rather than surrender. Fact is, the boy left in there with him, his nephew, Arch Wolf, had his hair catch afire, that's how hot it got."

Cap paused long enough to take another healthy swallow of the spiked coffee, then wiped his lips with a forefinger.

"First Arch come out, his hair aflame, and almost as quickly Ned runs out, Winchester blazing. He wasn't about to go down easy."

"Lord, God, but I do know that to be true," I said, remembering my run-in with Ned.

"That brave if crazy damn Indun come straight at us too. Didn't give us any recourse but to put him down, and that we did. Put him down. And down he will forever stay."

"Congratulations on that," I said.

Cap sat a while musing in silence and I didn't try to disturb his thoughts. Then he said, "You know we hauled ol' Ned back to Fort Smith and collected the reward of a thousand dollars. But by the time all expenses were paid and we divvied the leftover between us deputies, we each come out with seventy-four dollars. And it didn't come close to cleaning the stink of Ned's rotting corpse out of our nostrils."

He shook his head in dismay.

"You ever wonder why it is some deputies have crossed over to the other side of the law, like those Daltons and them?" he asked. "Well, right about there is your answer. A man risks his life against the most dangerous kind of killers and gone weeks at a time and ends up with pocket change for his troubles while another man can walk into a bank and walk out in five minutes with a sack full of cash money. Don't seem right."

"You thinking about going to the other side?" I said.

He looked at me a long silent moment then said, "I've thought about it. But then you end up like Ned and them: your corpse strapped to a door and pictures took of you to be sold for two bits apiece. How'd something like that be for your folks and loved ones, you to leave that as your legacy?"

"None too good I reckon."

"Wished to hell I could say Ned was the last of the badmen we had to run down, but he's far from it."

"We'll all be old and in our graves before we see the last of 'em," I said.

"Don't suppose you'd have any more coffee left in that pot? And some of that bug juice to go in it?"

I went and filled our cups and we killed another half hour in idle chat, then I watched him ride off in the hack he'd rented pulled by a spirited bay.

CHAPTER 9

"You ever see such poor country as this?" Sheriff Beeson said.

"Nope, can't say as I ever have," U.S. Deputy Marshal Tom Hueston replied, a chaw of tobacco the size of a billiard ball swollen in his cheek. He leaned and spat brown juice into the dry cold dust.

"And damn this wind too," he said.

Beeson rode with his fists balled in the pockets of his blanket coat. He'd forgotten to bring gloves. He was already hankering to get back to Dodge City.

"You think we'll find him at his cousin's?" he asked.

Again Tom spat more out of habit than need, then touched the back of his mouth with his wrist.

"I do believe we will. Rabbits always run to their hidey holes."

They'd been tracking Ol Yantis since the Spearville bank robbery there in Ford County, Beeson's county, and Beeson took it personal that they had been so bodacious to rob a bank in a county he was sheriff of. Besides, election time was nigh.

"I've heard stories about him and her," Hueston said.

"What sort of stories?"

"About them living like man and wife. Some say she's his cousin and others say his sister, or stepsister."

"Well, I'll be damned. You reckon they're true?"

"You know what they say: where there's smoke there's bound to be fire."

Beeson's horse snuffled and fought its bit, chewing it between its teeth, tossing its head, snorting and prancing its back feet.

"What's wrong with your horse?" the deputy said.

"Ah hell if I know, but may be that I don't ride it enough so it gets to be sort of wild between times. I don't care much for saddle riding no more. Prefer a hack."

"You think he'll put up a fight?"

"My horse?"

"No, Ol?"

"I think if he's cornered he might."

"You know him much?"

"Hardly at all. You?"

"Just what little I heard about him and that woman he lives with."

"Where'd you hear it?"

"I don't know. Wherever anybody hears anything. Just rumors is all."

"Well, if it's true, then I reckon a fellow like that would do just about anything, wouldn't you?"

The day was cold under a sad gray sky without promise of anything good in it and Ol went about stuffing wood chunks in the cast iron stove to get the fire stoked up again. It had almost burned out in the night. He was in his long handles still, barefooted, his black hair grown into wild wings as though something had frightened him.

The woman yet slept in the narrow bed, the blankets pulled up over her face so that she was just the shape of a woman beneath the blankets. Ol got down the coffee can and pumped water into a potash coffee pot with a blackened bottom from being fire-scorched. He added the coffee and set it atop a stove plate then found his makings and set at the table to fashion himself a shuck waiting for the coffee to boil. He had to get up again to get the box of Blue Diamond matches to light his cigarette and stubbed his big toe in the doing and cussed.

He struck one of the matches with his thumbnail and held the flame to the end of his cigarette, then blew it out and laid it on the table as he sat staring at the lump in the bed.

I ought not to be doing with her what I been doing all along, he thought. *It goes against nature but I can't seem to help it. It ain't like they is a trainload of women running all over the place like jackrabbits you can just catch you one.* He promised himself then and there he'd have a talk with her once she got up and about and had her morning coffee. Make her see they were sinning in a way God might not forgive.

Yes, sir, I'm gone set things right.

It wasn't long before the coffee began to percolate up in the glass dome and he stood and got himself a cup hanging from a peg on the wall and filled it and sat down again. He reached for the sugar bowl and spooned in a fair amount to sweeten the coffee and wished he had some cow's milk or cream to go in it, but he didn't.

"Someday I ain't gone live like this no more," he told himself, sipping his coffee and smoking his shuck and staring at the lump in the bed. "Someday I'm gone live right and have me a proper wife and stop all this foolishness and messing with Doolin and them boys too. Soon as I put me up a decent stake and get straightened around."

She stirred and turned over in the bed but did not awaken even though he was watching her intently. Sometimes when he did, she would awaken.

No, I'm gone get myself straightened around, maybe change my name if I have to and move away from all this. Might even go into the preaching business. They say a fellow can get by all right in the preaching business what with folks feeding him all the time and putting money in a basket for him to live on. Become one of them circuit riding preachers, go all over. Maybe meet me a pretty woman some-

wheres. When he got his thinking spigot turned on it flowed like a water of ideas.

Suddenly, he heard his name being shouted.

"Ol Yantis! It's the law: Sheriff Beeson of Ford County and Deputy Marshal Hueston from the Western District courts! We know you're in there and you best come on out with your hands up or suffer the consequences."

"Christ almighty," he muttered, spilling his coffee as he scrambled from the table to the window to peek out.

Two large mustachioed men sat their horses, Winchesters balanced over their pommels.

"What in the damn hell?"

The woman opened her eyes.

"Ol, who you talking to?"

"The laws!" he said harshly.

She sat up.

"The laws?"

"Right out there in the yard."

She scrambled from the bed and glanced out too.

"What do they want?"

"What do you think they want? How'd those sonsabitches find me, anyway?"

"If you don't come out in two minutes, we'll set fire to the place," one of them said. They wore their badges pinned to the front of their coats.

"Don't shoot!" he called. "I'll come forth. They's a woman in here!"

"You make sure your hands are empty, Ol."

"What will they do to you?" she said.

"Probably take me to the nearest jail, maybe hang me, maybe shoot me instead."

In this light he saw plainly how homely a gal she was, how grayish her skin, pitted too and her hair all athwart. He wanted to say something to her, to tell her he'd decided they had to stop living like they were living, but right now, he told himself, he had his hands full of trouble.

"Don't go out there, Ol," she said.

"I don't reckon I got no choice, less you want them to burn us out."

"I don't care. Let 'em. It don't matter to me, Ol."

He scrambled quickly for his trousers and got them on and buckled them tight around his waist, then tucked a short-barrel nickel-plated pistol with bird's-head grips down into the waistband at his spine.

"They'll kill you, Ol."

"Or I'll kill them," he said.

"I'm coming out, boys, don't shoot me now."

"Come on, we won't shoot you."

He glanced at her once more, said, "After this is over, you and me need to talk about something, Iona."

She nodded expectantly. What Ol couldn't know was that she had news to tell him as well: She was pregnant.

He went to the door and opened it slowly and stepped out, his hands partially raised, to show them they were empty.

They sat holding their rifles pointed at him.

"Don't shoot," he said, stepping gingerly into the cold yard dirt. "Goddamn you can see I ain't armed."

"Get down on your knees Ol while Tom here puts the manacles on you," Chalk Beeson ordered.

The other one started to dismount after shoving his rifle into his saddlesock, the leather creaking in the cold morning air.

Ol sank to his knees slowly, hands raised, thinking, *We'll just see how quick and brave you boys are, as the one walked toward him holding a pair of iron cuffs.*

He snatched around behind him and jerked the pistol free and fired two quick shots, but both missed their target.

The one still sitting his horse fired a slug from his Winchester that struck Ol like a hammer in his thigh, near his crotch, that caused him to scream like a whipped child. And in that same instant the one walking toward him drew his revolver and fired, striking Ol in the stomach. The .45-caliber slug ripped through Ol's intestines with jagged heat. It felt like he had swallowed acid and it caused him to wretch up his morning coffee. Ol's pistol spilled from his hand. "Christ!" he said. "Christ. You done killed me, you sons a bitches."

The one sitting his horse and the other one stood at the ready, hammers thumbed back, levers jacked.

"I'm quits," Ol struggled to say. "Please don't shoot me no more . . ."

"Reckon maybe you are quits," one of them said as they both now stood over him. From red eyes his tears spilled down his grubby cheeks and dripped into the pooling blood. It was like a thing had gotten inside of him, a thing with razor-sharp teeth that was eating at his guts, a thing he knew he couldn't ever get rid of.

He heard Iona wailing, calling, "Oh, God, Ollie!" Her voice sounded very far away and he tried looking over at her but the thing inside him wouldn't let him.

The lawmen loaded him into his own wagon and drove him into Orlando to the hotel since it was the nearest town. But there wasn't a doctor anywhere to be had to try and save him. Beeson and Hueston did their best to nurse him, but as spectators of other mortal wounds they both knew a man gutshot so bad as Ol Yantis that it was simply a matter of time.

Once they'd settled him on an old iron bed whose springs groaned, the lawmen took up watch in a pair of ladder-back chairs just outside in the hallway with its worn-out spit- and mud-stained carpet, their eyes hooded from weariness.

Iona had rode in with them and sat next to Ol's bed all night long, whispering and weeping.

Ol's fevered dreams caused him to mutter in strange tongues like the folks who went to those traveling preacher tents and got saved. He had dreams wherein he saw fiery devils dancing about and silver dimes raining from the sky, more than a man could stuff in his pockets. He heard the thundering of horse hooves and saw his dead kin standing out in the yard waving to him. He tossed about on the bed and Iona did her best to sooth his troubled spirit, damping rags in a bucket of fetched water to lay upon his forehead and pack his bloody wounds. The rags turned first pink, then dark crimson, and outside the hard wind rattled the windowpanes and roared up the street like something seeking retribution on the unfortunate, of which Ol was now one.

And at last when the first light of new morning entered the room and the wind abated, Ol sighed and murmured, "I . . . I . . ." Then sighed once more deeply and ceased his breathing.

"He's dead," Iona whispered the announcement, her eyes blood red, her pitted cheeks trailing wet streaks. She looked near death herself, so wan and bloodless.

"Yes, ma'am," Chalk Beeson said as if he already knew. "We wished it could have been some other way, but it wasn't."

"Whatever will I do now without Ollie?"

The lawmen exchanged looks but said nothing.

She went out of the hotel and they watched from the window in Ol's room as she mounted the wagon's seat and took up the reins of the horse team and drove off back toward her and Ollie's homestead.

"There goes one sad and miserable soul," said Beeson. "I feel pity for her."

"You reckon it was true the things they said about him and her being kin?" Hueston said, pulling a shabby coverlet over the dead fugitive.

"I don't know," Beeson said. "Could be all she was to him

was just a friend, a woman who loved him and there's something to be said for that, I reckon, having someone love you no matter what sort of a fellow you are."

"Well, whatever it was, it ain't no more."

"One down and two more to go," Chalk Beeson said.

"Maybe for that bank robbery in Spearville," Deputy Hueston said, "but a lot more'n that all told for me and the other deputies, at least."

"Reckon I don't envy you boys none, traipsing all over the Nations in search of these miscreants."

"Reckon I don't either. Come on let's apply for the reward money. I'll need some funds to get back home again."

"I got flat pockets too."

Off they went. One more Oklahombre to be put in the ground and plenty more still walking the earth. A lawman's work wasn't ever going to be finished, they both knew. Not in a thousand years or more. There'd always be work for a man with a gun and a badge, just as there would always be men willing to be their own sort of law, no badge needed, thank you very much.

Bitter Creek Newcomb dangled a length of rope out front of Mary Pierce's hotel there in Ingalls waiting for Doolin to arrive. The day was not unpleasant even if cold, what with the sun helping to stave off much of the chill. The wind had died considerable during the night. Newcomb had staggered back to his room with a floozy he paid a dollar for the privilege. They'd shared a bottle of popskull and he watched her undress in the flickering of a bedstand's lamp. She was older than he liked them, but hell, he was a long ways from Rose and back home again. He liked to tell the other boys, "You turn out the lights and they pretty much all look the same, feel the same, do the same, and it all ends up the same. It's the morning you got to be braced for." Then laugh like hell.

When he awoke, she was gone, thankfully, and he'd dressed

and gone up the street in search of breakfast grub and found it at some café or other. He ordered eggs and grits and fried fatback and coffee and swallowed two cups before his meal arrived and washed the food down with two more cups, then went and sat out front of the hotel, dangling the rope, trying to get it to loop itself, an old cowboy trick he'd learned months and months ago from none other than Emmitt Dalton. Emmitt was a trickster.

Dangling that rope he thought of Emmitt and tried picturing him suffering with a load of buckshot in him, and if he lived, facing a lifetime of prison, no doubt about it. And if he didn't live . . . well, there was always that.

It was close to noon when Doolin arrived and dismounted and wrapped the reins of his horse around the hitch rail.

"Wondering if you'd make it," Newcomb said.

"I sent word to Tulsa Blake to round up some of the boys and meet us here," Bill said, taking residence in the empty chair next to Newcomb's.

"When they coming?"

"Should be any time today, I hope."

"You got a job in mind, then?"

"Yeah."

Bitter Creek continued to dangle the rope while Bill made himself a shuck, the wind every now and then jumping up and gusting hard enough to snatch some of the tobacco flakes out of the trough of paper he'd formed.

"What the hell we sitting out here for?" Bill said with irritation in his voice.

"What's stuck in your craw?"

"Nothing," Bill said, twisting off the ends of a poorly made cigarette and fumbling around in his coat pocket for a match. Finding none, he searched around inside his waistcoat pockets.

"Got word they killed Ol," he said at last, having found a

single match and lighting his smoke with it.

Newcomb stopped dangling the rope.

"What? When?"

"A few days ago. Tracked him to his and Iona's. Said he didn't go down easy."

"Well shitfire, anyway."

"Put his corpse on display in the undertaker's window. Said they dressed him in a white shirt and checkered trousers and combed his hair with rosewater. Said the undertaker sold snippets of his hair for fifty cents and a newspaperman two dollars to take his photograph."

Bitter Creek grunted, said, "How'd Iona take it?"

Doolin shrugged, looking up and down both ways the street in hopes the others might show soon.

"Reckon she took it hard, you know how it was with her and Ol."

"Goddamn but the way they do us," Bitter Creek said, thinking of the hair snipping.

"Let's go find us a cup of coffee or something," Bill said. "This shit-ass weather is enough to put a fellow in a bad mood."

"I done had four or five cups. Whyn't we opt for a beer?"

"Kinda early for drinking," Doolin said checking the time on his nickel-plated Waltham railroad watch.

"Well, it might be too early here, but I bet it's late enough somewhere."

Doolin did not protest.

As if wolves drawn to a carcass, they arrived one by one: Tulsa Jack Blake, "Dynamite" Dick Clifton, George "Red Buck" Weightman, "Little Bill" Raidler, and to the surprise of some, Bill Dalton, the last of the ill-fated brothers.

They rode into town like bedraggled travelers, a cadre of well-armed men on winter-coated horses, the riders dressed in heavy jackets with kerchiefs knotted around their throats and sweat-stained Stetsons with curled brims tugged down to the tops of their ears.

They were, the lot of them, waiting there at the hotel when Bill Doolin and Bitter Creek Newcomb returned late that evening from a day of drinking and card playing and whore flirtation with whatever whores were about. By the time they arrived they were as cheery as a sewing machine salesman who'd been visiting farm wives all day.

"Hail, hail the gang's all here," Newcomb said at the sight of the others.

The waiters were a grim-faced bunch, and none more grim-faced than Bill Dalton, eldest brother of the dead and wounded Daltons. He had still not gotten over the death of his kin, the wounding of Emmitt, his mother's tears at the loss of her sons, his promise to avenge their killings.

They took the hotel's available rooms and Doolin told them about Ol Yantis, warning how the law wasn't ever going to quit coming after them no matter what and that he intended to make it worth the law's time by knocking over as many banks and trains and whatever other places had money in it as he could before heading himself, with Edith, to Mexico, or someplace the laws couldn't catch up with them.

"They'll by god reckon with us or we'll reckon with them, but either way, those laws are going to track each and every one of us down and put us on the wrong side of the dirt if they can. I don't aim to see that happen."

He lifted the hat off his head and held it dramatically over his heart and said, "Now let's have a moment of kindness for Ol," to which the others traded befuddled glances, some with sly grins. In their mind Ol Yantis was a flea-bitten hardcase who diddled his own sister or cousin or whatever kin she was to him, and none of them figured a moment of kindness in his honor would carry much weight with his maker.

When Bill Doolin plopped his hat back on his head they all nodded in silent accession and passed around a bottle of bug juice one of them had taken from his pocket.

"You're right about the laws not giving up on us," Tulsa Blake said. He was one of Bill's most ardent supporters. Some of the others might have called him a sycophant if they'd known what the word meant. None of them did, but they all sort of knew it when they saw it in action.

"Winter'll be on us soon anyway," Doolin added. "Soon the roads will be clogged with snow and the cold so bad it will cut like a straight razor. We best make hay while the ol' sun shines."

"Mighty poetic," Tulsa Blake said.

A few of the others groaned and said, "Keep passing that bottle of Doc Tolver around, my blood's been cold for a month already."

Somebody asked, "Anybody ever been to Florida? I hear it's warm all year round down there."

"They got snakes the size of your leg," somebody else said.

Evening light was fading outside the windows of the hotel, the streets were growing quiet with proper folks heading home to supper, to warm fires and featherbeds.

"How do you get there?" Red Buck said.

"Get where?" Dynamite Dick said.

"Florida."

"Hell if I know. I reckon you catch a train is how. That or ride your horse."

"Reckon the train would make more sense," Little Bill Raidler chimed in. He was currently in possession of the bottle and the smidgen left in the bottom. He put it to his mouth, swallowed, and held it at arm's length looking at it.

"Another dead soldier," he said.

"We ought to go and get us some more," Bitter Creek suggested.

And so they did.

They drank well into the night, till the stars salted the black sky with some falling from the heavens to unknown places on the earth. Doolin and Tulsa Blake had stepped outside to relieve themselves, both of them looking skyward and shivering in the cold.

"I'd like someday to go and find me one of them stars," Blake said. "I bet it would bc good luck, or maybe worth some kind of money or something."

"How the hell you gone find one?" Bill said, feeling giddy as a schoolgirl from all the whiskey they'd drunk.

"I reckon there's some sort of trick to it, small as they are," Blake answered.

"Well you be sure and let me know when you find one."

"How's Edith?"

Bill glanced over at him.

"I don't care much for you asking after my wife, you holding your pecker in your hand."

"Well hell, Bill, you know I didn't mean nothing by it. I'm just relieving myself is all."

Bill threw back his head and howled. The suddenness of the howling caused Blake to spray his boots then curse his poor aim. Doolin laughed like a crazy man.

"Woooeee! But ain't we hell on wheels! I feel like I could hang the moon."

"Me too," said Blake.

It was that brief moment of camaraderie that men of the same nature sometimes share. It made them feel good to be in each other's company.

★ ★ ★ ★ ★

Heck Thomas was playing whist with Chris Madsen and Bill Tilghman when word was delivered about the death of Ol Yantis. It was Ol's sister, Iona, who delivered it in person.

"I want to file a complaint," she said.

"About what exactly, ma'am?" the big Dane Madsen said.

"About the laws gunning down my brother, Ol Yantis. I'm his sister and I want to file a damn complaint!"

The three lawmen looked at each other, unsure of exactly what to make of this unhandsome woman made more unhandsome by her angry demeanor. She seemed to the trio about like a wet hen for all the squawking she was doing, but for too little feathers. Her face was ruddy from a raw wind that had searched out the town of Lawton and all those in it. Presently it was spitting snow and threatening worse judging by the bruised and swollen sky that looked as though it had been in a tremendous fistfight with God and lost.

The wind rattled the tin of roofs not nailed down tightly and rippled water in the watering troughs. It scattered grit like buckshot.

It was news to the lawmen, Ol Yantis's death. They had not received any official word as of yet, had been in fact discussing leaving off the chase for any further miscreants due to the coming weather. It was Tilghman who'd suggested it, saying, "Those boys will all den up, I suspect, like they usually do comes winter, and it wouldn't hurt any of us to den up too with our wives. I'm sure they'd appreciate having their husbands home with them and we'd appreciate it too."

"Yours maybe," Heck grunted. "I doubt mine will."

It was an open secret that Heck's wife had been giving him fits and ten sorts of grief about almost everything, but mostly the hard frontier life and his long absences.

"Isabelle is packing to head back home with the children.

Can't say I blame her. Wife of a lawman ain't no sort of life for a woman."

A silence fell over them when he said that. Now here was this rather homely woman whom they all three had heard the most salacious sorts of rumors about demanding to file a complaint for the killing of her outlaw brother.

"Tell you what, ma'am," Heck said, taking the pipe from between his teeth and setting it in a glass ashtray. "You write it out, what you want to say, and I'll see that it gets to the proper authority."

"And who would that be?" she demanded.

"Why, Judge Parker, of course," he said.

She studied his features to see if she could detect about him any sort of whimsy, whether he might be making a fool of her. But she could not. She reached into her reticule and took out a folded paper scrawled with blue ink and handed it to him.

"It's all right there, every jot and tittle," she said. "Just as I seen it with my own eyes, how them dirty lawdogs assassinated my brother when all they had to do was arrest him. He was on his knees in the yard, his hands in the air, and they shot him down like they would a rabid coyote. I want justice!"

"Yes, ma'am, I'll see the judge gets this."

The Dane was privately thinking, *Well, knowing Ol Yantis as I do, he was just about like a rabid coyote that needed putting down and I ain't too awful upset that he was.*

By now her face was as stormy as the sky outside, her eyes as cold as the coldest wind. She was wide-mouthed and wide-hipped and Heck reckoned that maybe if a fellow turned out the lights in the night he might could pretend enough to get the job done, a blind man maybe with a good drunk on. But then berated his own thinking. *How long's it been since I had even a homely woman? I ought not to judge this one, regardless of her looks.*

She turned then, not knowing what else she could do. She'd

gone with the expectation to be laughed at, to be discarded, her complaint about the way they'd done Ol dirty. But that fellow with the sandy moustaches and big white Stetson hat perched at a jaunty angle on his head had let her sap run its course and treated her halfway respectable. The other two had sat silent, looking down at their card hands, meek as children.

Well, I reckon I gave them a good piece of my mind, didn't I? Then, whether it was the raw wind or just plain bone-deep sorrow, tears stung her eyes. Ol wasn't even yet cold in his grave but it was like he'd been forever gone away from her, the house felt empty without him, the bed some cold. Every time she looked at his empty boots by the bedside she wept a little bit more. He might not have been no king or nothing, but to her he was all she ever had in the way of a man and probably all she would ever have, a woman well into her middle age. She didn't need to look in the mirror to know what men thought of her looks. Ol never seemed to care.

She was, with every passing minute, stricken with greater and greater grief. Her brief elation at having presented her case to the lawmen on behalf of Ol had fled from her as swiftly as a small bird before the winter's wind.

She found herself standing at the train depot. Just standing there as if frozen to the earth with grievous doubt as to what the next moment held for her.

The station man wrapped on the window and raised it a notch and called out to her: "Would you like to purchase a ticket for the train, Miss?"

His eyes were small blue marbles pressed into the dough of his face.

"No," she said. "I was just passing on."

"Oh," he said and shut the window closed again.

She did not know why or where she was going, but began walking along the track, the worn soles of her button shoes crunching on the cinders that lay between the ties, the cold wind lifting from them the scent of creosote.

It was too late when the engineer spotted her, the train coming in hot, for it was already nearly an hour late. He shoved the brake's handle hard as he could, screaming at the fireman, "Holy God, they's a woman on the tracks!"

The fireman stopped shoveling and stood and turned around and leaned out and he saw her too. A woman all in black, like a haint. The engineer pulled the whistle chord and sent forth a shriek to warn her. But she didn't act like she even heard it.

The large steel wheels grated against the slender steel tracks and together they raised a screaming warning that would have roused even the dead, but not the woman.

Even from quarter of a mile distance the station manager could hear the awful noise and ran out to see the cause of the train's racket, figured it was about to jump the rails. He barely caught a glimpse of the woman before the black behemoth of steel and iron and chuffing smoke swallowed her into its maw.

"God be!" he said to no one there. "God be."

Heck Thomas still had Iona's grievance letter in his pocket when he heard it announced by some townsman who'd come in that a woman had been run over and killed on the train tracks.

"Nobody knows who she was," the fellow said. "And there's not enough of her to even try and figure it out."

Heck took out the letter and set it on the table and Chris Madsen and Bill Tilghman studied it with their eyes and nobody said a thing, but they ceased playing cards nonetheless.

Every time somebody new came in the cold wind came in with them and they had to force the door shut to close it out. And every time, no matter who it was said the same thing:

"Damn but ain't it raw?" Then: "You all hear about some woman getting run over by the train?"

Heck and them stood and walked out, leaving the letter of complaint there on the table next to the deck of playing cards and the next person to come in let a draft of air in with them that swept the letter clean from the table and blew it lost into the stove's woodbox.

Chapter 10

The game's not half over and too much blood already, boys, too much blood.

When I came home, Isabelle was packed and gone, and so were my baby children. The entire house was empty and when I walked my footsteps rang hollow upon the boards. Even the curtains she had taken from the windows so that there was nothing to stop the winter light from coming in, begrimed as the glass was, a light no more passionate that the cold arms of the dead wrapped around you.

Onliest thing left was my clothes hanging there in the closet we once shared, she and I. Our bed was without a coverlet, just the bare tick mattress I sat upon and held my head in my hands.

First I was sad and then I got angry at her for doing it, coward like, while I was away instead of waiting until I got back and the two of us hashing it out. I admit, I cussed her good on account of it. Called her every vile name in the book, names I won't repeat on paper. I knew it was mostly my fault she was gone and took our kids with her. I knew it but it didn't stanch my anger at her.

There was just one other thing of hers I found: a note on the kitchen table.

Dear Heck,

I am sorry to have left you like this, it wasn't the way I wanted it to end. But you left me little choice. How much longer did you expect I could stand to be left alone in this horrible place with five children to raise as if they had no father at all, you gone all the time?

Over the course of our marriage you come home just long enough to put me with child again, then off you go in chase of your wild criminals, you and your band of brothers, as you call them. They seem closer to you than your own family. You seem to care for them more than your own flesh and blood.

I can no longer abide such hardship, nor can the children who all the time ask about their father, when is he coming home, is he dead, been killed somewhere. They cry for you and I got no answers to give them. In many ways it would be easier if I could tell them that you had died and were in heaven. At least then they could understand your absences more.

I'm sorry if you find all this hurtful, but if so, then you know a little of how hurtful I've found our years together, the hardships of raising your children practically alone, the poor pay you earn leaving us all too little to practically live on, the bickering that seems to have taken the place of what once was a harbor of love.

Goodbye, Heck. Take care of yourself. Isabelle.

Boy, reading those words was worse than being stabbed in the heart. It knocked me right down to where I got on my horse and rode to town and got good and drunk and stayed good and drunk nearly a week. Or maybe it was two.

I sure did miss my kids, but I honestly can say I did not so much miss my wife. She was right about most if not all of what she said about me being gone too much of the time, and the rest of it too.

I'd come home after being gone sometimes for weeks at a time and I couldn't wait to get her undressed. Not so much because I loved her, but because I am a man with a man's needs and it was her duty to provide her wifely duties to me, just as it was my husbandly duties to provide her shelter and food.

But always, always did I pay the price afterward because all we did was bicker and fight, mostly over money, me being gone, not there to share the household duties, to be a father to my brood. Got so after a time of being a lawman and loving the work like I did, I forgot how to do most of those things. Got so I liked being gone because it made coming home to her that much sweeter and I always knew that it wouldn't be long before I was called away again.

I thought as a wife, it was her duty to raise the children and keep the house and do all the other things wives were supposed to do. I never asked her to work outside the house and earn pay. Earning wages was a man's duty, my duty, and that's what I did.

But she broke under the bit and run off with my kids and it put an anger toward her deep into my heart and I hated her for it.

I half thought she wanted me to go after her and bring her back, but I never would lower my pride to do it, no matter how much I loved and missed those kids. I wasn't about to let her hold me hostage.

My goddamn pride, that's all it was.

I guess that, and my hands didn't yet have enough blood on them.

The Nations was still wild with all the miscreants robbing and raping and killing innocent folks and somebody had to try and stop them, to put them out of business.

If I didn't do it, who would?

That's the one question I would have asked her if she'd ever let me.

She never let me.

CHAPTER 11

Winter ravaged the land with biting wind, terrible cold, and snow that sometimes drifted deep enough to clog the roads between towns and settlements. It howled and moaned like something badly wounded, like the hounds of hell someone said in a saloon in Sapulpa. But folks were always saying such things every winter, just like they commented about the unrelenting heat in summer, the cyclones and wild fires and flooding rains when they came. A man's opinion might not count for much most days, but at least the forces of Mother Nature gave him something to opine on among others who had their own opinions to which all could agree. At least holding court on the weather didn't lead to fistfights like it might when it came to politics.

Cowhands that rode the range hunkered down in airy line shacks they winterized with old newspapers and passed the tedious time playing whist and dominoes while there was yet light to see by, and when there wasn't, they lay abed at night listening to the windsong and wondered how many days more would they have to wait until it let up. Some few gave thought to suicide when they thought overly long of sweethearts so far away or of the warm sunshine of south Texas. And some few did more than merely think about it. Here and there if a fellow listened long and hard enough, he might well hear a single gunshot followed by wintry silence.

Harlots in a Tulsa brothel stroked the backs of their pet

housecats, their fingers searching through the soft fur down to the delicate bones of the felines as if searching out some secret of contentment contained therein. Business was always slow in the worst of the winter and there was much time to reflect and grieve of childhood times back on farms in Ohio and Indiana, of pony rides and baking bread with their mothers, of first kisses from first beaus, and moonlight hay rides down by the river on a summer's eve so near perfect it seemed impossible to be so happy.

Men drank to excess just to pass the time and in their drinking became belligerent with one another, or, as some observed, simply taken in the head with a madness unable to be explained. Winter's light made even the sun seem made of cold hammered metal.

Such brutal cold turned even the slyest man irritable and itching for a fight, and fight they did almost over anything. A tin drummer in Ardmore got into an argument with a broke dick cowboy over a cup of coffee and gunfire erupted as suddenly and loudly as a thunderclap. The drummer grasped his neck trying to stanch the jet of blood from an artery the cowboy's bullet had nicked and collapsed to the floor while the cowboy who shot him returned to his drinking and negotiated a price with a saloon girl to get her into a bed more for the warmth than for sexual pleasure.

One furious storm caught a boy out trying to go from house to privy. The air had turned completely white from the wind-driven snow and he became lost in it. In his last moments alive he cried for someone to come help him but his cries were drowned out by the howling winds. His body was not found until the spring melt.

Near Lawson, Bill Doolin holed up too as did the other gang members, Bill with his young wife Edith and Newcomb with Rose. The others with whoever would have them. The Dunn brothers continued to take illegal meat for their butcher shop while waiting to go on the warpath come spring in search of wanted men they could collect bounty on.

Bill also had plans for the coming spring. He wanted to rob more banks and trains. He wanted to get his hands on as much money as he could before the laws caught up to him as they had begun to do others. He told himself he wasn't getting any younger, for he already felt old and not yet forty. This time he promised himself he'd not spend most of it on foolish things, but rather find a place, perhaps in Old Mexico where he and Edith could live out their days in peace, having children. The idea of going to South America as other outlaw brethren had talked about held no allure for him. Mexico seemed plenty far enough.

"I was thinking maybe sometime soon we'll all move to Mexico, your papa and you and me," he said while Edith finished fixing lunch for the two of them.

"But Bill," she said. "We'd have to learn the language."

Bill was feeding the stove chunks of split wood. He used the poker to position it around then closed the door with its isinglass little windows and slipped the latch.

"I don't imagine it would be all that hard. They say all it does is sunshine every day," Bill said. "Bill Dalton said he lived down there for a time, said it's quite wonderful and the land is cheap."

"Why'd he come back to Oklahoma then, if it was all so wonderful?"

More and more lately Edith had herself grown quarrelsome, it seemed to him. Spoke up about his absences.

"To avenge the murder of his brothers," Doolin said with muted but growing irritation.

"Murder! Why I thought they were killed trying to rob banks."

"Well, they were, but Bill looks at it like it was murder, plain and simple."

"Lord be. It sounds to me as if it was justified, them trying to steal those folks' money."

Bill simply looked at her as he sat down at the table between them and sipped his hot coffee.

"Is there something wrong with your coffee?" she asked as she saw the way he was treating it, how he tore off a chunk of fresh baked bread and began dunking it in the coffee and eating it that way without drinking it too much.

"No wonder you're as thin as you are," she said, watching him eating his coffee-dunked bread. "Why don't I fix you a proper meal?"

"This'll do," he said.

He watched her watching it snow, the wind blowing the snow slantwise so that it obliterated everything outside, the barn and sheds and privy. Her garden spot was crusted over with snow and ice.

"I hope papa didn't get caught out in this storm," she said in a papery voice. "I hope he made it to Tahlequah okay."

"I'm sure he did," Doolin said, swiping coffee dew from his moustaches and patting the dribble from his chin with his shirt cuff.

Only a month into the hard winter season and already he had grown restless. The money in the tin box under the bed was getting low as well. The last job they'd pulled netted less than a thousand dollars. Split five ways came to two hundred each. Doolin had bought himself a new shirt, hat, and rifle. He had bought Edith three new dresses and a pair of bone gray buttoned-up shoes in a store in Eufaula. He didn't know her dress size but had to guess and guessed it to be about the same size as the young lady who waited on him. Had her hold the chosen dresses up in front of her.

She was pretty. Had red hair and green eyes and an Irish brogue. Cute as a button. He couldn't resist. They spent the night together. She had freckles splattered across her chest. She proved to be wild as a bucking bronc once he opened the chute, figured it was the hard cider they'd drank together from a bottle set by the bed.

He thought about her now, drinking his coffee and eating his dunked bread. He knew he ought to feel bad about it, his unfaithfulness, but something in him didn't allow it. He thought of her with longing and pleasure. How hard she kissed him and rode him down. He told Tulsa Blake, "I was rode hard and put away wet." Blake grinned like a coon eating cob corn. Said, "I wished I had your ways with women, Bill."

It had been a month since the first snow came blowing in on razor-sharp winds. Now he had to go out every day and chop ice off the water trough so the horses could drink. The snow crunched under his boots. The wind chaffed his hands and reddened his face as he did chores. It burned his ears as he mucked out the horse stalls, pitched hay down from the mow. His labored breathing created small frosted clouds that iced in his beard. His kneebones ached.

The desperate wind swayed through the trees, causing them to creak like saddle leather, and the spiderwork of streams froze over so that he had to chop the ice on them too when he needed to haul water in galvanized pails up to the house.

Once while chopping more kindling the axhead slipped and whanged off his shinbone flatsided. He jumped and cussed every square inch of Oklahoma. Boy he sure hated this winter life, the brutal work, the dull sameness of each day, the constant struggle just to do things that needed doing.

Sometimes he'd take Edith to bed several times a day just for something to do. She never complained, but he could tell she'd just as soon be doing something else. She wasn't so eager and willing as with that redheaded gal in Eufaula.

When not doing chores or bedding Edith, he would sit in the

rocker before the fireplace and doze while trying to read the latest issue of *Police Gazette, McCall's,* or going through the *Sears Roebuck* catalogue.

Edith would call him to dinner or supper and he'd eat and sometimes they'd talk about one thing or another and sometimes they wouldn't. He knew she wanted to ask him more details about his life and work, exactly how he and the others got the money to buy cattle to resell, or the horses. Because it didn't seem to her possible to come in with a pocket full of money as much as he did sometimes. And her papa had wondered too.

But he had told her it was just man's work, the countryside was full of maverick cattle if a man was willing to work to round them up, and nothing very much interesting about it all.

"It's just plain old hard work," he said. "Nothing quite so exciting as what you might think."

She turned from watching the slantwise snow and said, "I read Ol Yantis was killed by lawmen. You were friends of his weren't you, Bill?"

"Yes," he said. "I knew Ol. He must have done something bad for to be murdered by the laws."

"The newspaper said he was part of a gang that robbed a bank in Kansas."

He stopped dunking his bread and looked at her in a way that let her know she was treading on ice more thin and dangerous than what formed itself over the cattle pond.

"Well," he said finally, "Ol sometimes ran with a bad bunch and maybe he did what the papers said, or maybe he didn't. The laws and the newspapers don't always get things right, Edith."

"I'm just surprised you didn't mention it," she said.

"Didn't mention it because I didn't know nothing about it."

He knew she was waiting for him to say something implicating, but he instead returned to concentrating on his sopping breakfast of bread and coffee.

"Oh, I wish the wind would stop just once in a while," she said. "It has my nerves frayed."

He rose from the table and went to the cupboard and took down a bottle of Old Tub and poured a half inch in a glass and said, "Take you some of this, it will soothe you right down."

"But, Bill, I'm a Christian."

"Hell, even the Lord drank a little wine now and then. I reckon he didn't have it none too easy either and had him a little now and then to ease his troubled mind."

He said it with such conviction and a winning smile she did not refuse him but swallowed what was in the glass and made a face.

"Just give it a second or two," he said.

"It's warm going down."

"Shows it's working."

"Oh, my," she said.

"Come sit down at the table," he said, guiding her to a chair.

After a few moments she said, "Mmm, that's quite a lovely feeling it gives you. Makes me somewhat lightheaded."

He thought again of the redheaded gal and was bestirred by the thought of her, the image burned into his memory of her nakedness, the sound of her gay laughter. Those damn freckles all over her chest.

"Maybe we should go and lay down a bit and take a nap," he said.

"Why, Bill, we just got out of bed."

"I'm just restless is all."

"I know it," she said. "It's this weather."

"Well, I best go out and do the chores," he said, standing away from the table and taking his mackinaw from a peg by the rear door that led out into a summer kitchen that still held the scent of autumn apples.

She watched him carefully because her head was slightly dizzy. Watched him buckle each buckle then put on his hat, its brim curled to a shape of his liking, its crown sweat-stained. His new hat he recently bought, still in a box up in the closet. Said it would be his go-to-meeting hat someday soon.

He tugged on a pair of rough leather gloves then went out, closing the door behind him and cutting off the inrushing wind.

She sat alone, wondering, *What is this life we live? What's it worth? What's it for? We are born and we grow old and we die and it makes not a whit of difference. We are forgotten and our bones turn to dust and once more we are of the earth from whence we came, made with spit and mud.* She stood and went to the cupboard and took the bottle down again and poured more into her glass.

The whiskey made her sleepy, eased her troubled mind.

CHAPTER 12

Winter's grip seemed an eagle's talon against the flesh and time crawled through day after day of the same bleakness, with barren trees and black cold creeks snaked through the land and a wind that shook and shivered through every living creature and building. January seemed colder than December and the first days of February colder still.

Doolin had the fidgets. Felt like he was going to come clear out of his skin.

He finally couldn't take just hanging around doing nothing any longer and saddled a horse and rode to Cowboy Flats. The wind stung his face and hands like whiplashes, and everywhere he looked the ground was covered in white and twice his horse slipped and nearly fell on the ice-slicked road.

Oh, how he cursed the winter. He needed a good stiff pull of some popskull, maybe two, and plan some jobs once the weather broke, to be among his kind, Bitter Creek Newcomb and Tulsa Jack Blake and them.

By the time he arrived and tied off out front of the hotel he was nearly frozen. His hands and knees were stiff and he moved like an old man just getting out of the saddle and into the hotel.

The clerk recognized him and said that the others of his acquaintance were over to the saloon. He stood for a minute by the woodstove in the center of the lobby warming his hands first and then his backside.

"Sure is beastly out, ain't it?" the clerk said.

"Like a son of a bitch," Doolin replied.

His ears stung from the cold and he half wondered if they weren't frostbit. He dreaded having to go back outside and into the blistering wind.

"Was some fellows come and got your friends to go over to the saloon with them," the clerk said.

"What fellows would that be?" Doolin said, suddenly alert to trouble.

The clerk shrugged. He was young and bookish peering over gold-rimmed spectacles, small agate eyes the size of marbles.

"Why I don't rightly know, sir. Just two pretty hard-looking fellows.

Doolin raised the collar of his coat and tugged down his hat tighter and forced himself to go out. Head down, he crossed the wide street walking as fast as he could, his knees yet too stiff to run, and made the saloon.

The light inside was weak. He had to stand there a moment letting his eyesight adjust until at last he spotted the boys, way in the back gathered around a pair of tables, their backsides to the last of three potbelly stoves that ran down the center of the room.

He unbuttoned his coat for easier access to the revolver tucked down in his waistband. It had hard rubber grips and a short barrel. He didn't know what to expect, who the fellows were the clerk had mentioned, what trouble might be afoot.

When he drew near, Tulsa Jack was the first to take notice of him and said loudly, "Well look what the cat's dragged in!" Gave a whoop.

The others looked up too.

Instantly he recognized the two strangers: Crawford Goldsby, the one they called Cherokee Bill, and Henry Starr. Both men were wanted for various crimes in the Nations and Oklahoma. The last time he'd seen either was over near Nowata not long after they'd stolen some horses and shot a fellow.

"Howdy, Bill," said the more gregarious Goldsby. Cherokee Bill was like an oversized kid, youthful face, large of body.

Doolin nodded. His gaze naturally went to the blade face of Henry Starr. Both men were halfbloods and Doolin didn't much trust either. He just believed you couldn't trust a blood overly much as you could a white fellow.

"Didn't expect to see you till spring," Bitter Creek Newcomb said, an unlit stogie in the corner of his mouth.

"Just needed to get out of the house for a while," Doolin said.

"You picked a hell of a day for a ride," Goldsby said, his big happy face staring up from beneath his sombrero hat.

"One's the same as another," Doolin replied.

"Grab you a chair," Tulsa Blake said.

"I'm going to warm my insides first."

Doolin walked to the bar and ordered a bottle set before him and a glass. He aimed on taking his time. The place was crowded with others, men who had no home or didn't want to be there. And of course the saloon gals were working the boys, trying to get them to peel off a dollar or two from their rolls. In this light it was hard to tell if they were pretty or only half so, not that it mattered. Everyone in the place seemed a little desperate.

His mind was elsewhere, restless, feeling guilty he hadn't provided Edith a better life, knew that she most likely suffered in silence, silence born out of her love and faithfulness for him. He didn't even know what she saw in him, the way he was, the way she was.

One of the hurdy-gurdy gals sidled up to him and said, "Buy a gal a drink, cowboy?"

"Not today, little Missy."

She gave him an awful sour look. He ignored her, kept watch of himself, his reflection, in the back-bar mirror. What he saw looking back at him was a roughcut ex-cowboy, now an outlaw, sporting a gun and an outlaw's heart.

Being an outlaw was like having a bad habit. You wanted to rid yourself of it, but there was simply too much pleasure in the money side of it. Where else was a man of his qualifications and education going to make so much money at one time while doing so little work for it?

He didn't know.

Newcomb came over, said, "You all right, Bill?"

"Just anxious to get started again. This damnable weather seems like it wants to drag on forever."

"Well, look at it this way, Bill. We don't move, the law don't move, either. The snow and the cold don't care which side of the fence you're on. They're holed up just like we are."

They drank whiskey and lapsed into silence.

A pair of Indians in white men's clothing—gingham shirts and denim jeans—came in and stepped to the end of the bar and ordered whiskey.

"You ain't supposed to be in here," the barkeep said.

"Why ain't we?" one of the Indians said, his voice raspy and harsh. He wore his hair in a long braided tail that reached near to his waist. The crown of his hat had a sizable hole in it. But none of it seemed to matter.

"Can't you read?" the barkeep said, pointing at a sign with his bulbous nose.

"Sure we can read," the one said. "What about that whiskey?"

"No skins!" the barkeep said, now pointing with his finger at the sign, the second line down: REDS, NIGGERS AND CHINAMEN NOT ALLOWED." It was right below the line that read: "NO UNESCORTED WOMEN."

The Indian stared at it a moment then said grievously, "I ain't no damn red nigger or no Chinaman either one. And I sure as hell ain't no unescorted woman. Now put a bottle of that popskull on the bar or I'm gone do something harsh."

With the subtlest of movements the barkeep made to act like he was going to do as they'd ordered, but instead of a bottle of liquor, he came up with a sawed-off shotgun and aimed it at them.

"You sure got a mouth on you, boy. You don't clear out I'm going to decorate the room with your damn dirty blood!"

Doolin took this in with only mild interest. Fights in bars were as common an occurrence as fleas on a hound.

The room was quiet enough that everybody in it could hear the double click of the shotgun's rabbit ear hammers being thumbed back.

"Well, shit," the Indian said. "What's it take to get a drink in this chickenshit town anyway!"

It was a rhetorical question, though nobody would have known what it was called. The thing that mattered was the barkeep had the advantage over the skins and even a damn thirsty fool knew it wasn't worth dying over, whiskey wasn't.

They backed on out of the place and rattled the doors shut hard. The barkeep shook his head as he replaced the shotgun below the bar after easing the hammers down.

"Damn trash," he muttered and poured himself a stiff one.

Whatever it was itching under Doolin's skin had eased itself somewhat and he turned and bid adieu to the others.

"You leaving so soon?" Tulsa Blake said.

"Got no reason to stay other than to watch you boys lose your pocket change and catch the pox off'n one of these hurdy-gurdy gals."

Laughter.

Bill stepped out into the frigid air.

The saddle leather was cold and hard.

I don't reckon it's ever going to get spring, Bill said to the horse as he turned him out to the road leading home again. The sun had broken through the leaded sky and now sparkled so brightly in the snow it hurt his eyes. He fumbled in his coat pocket for the spectacles with the smoked glass lenses, then realized when he couldn't find them that he must have left them at the house.

So he rode with his head down, his eyes squinted, the cold running through his veins like ice water.

He hadn't gone a block up the street when the two Indians stepped out in front of his horse.

"Say, white man, how 'bout you buying us some liquor in that saloon since that son of a bitch won't serve us?"

Doolin sat there peering down at them. He'd seen their likes plenty of times before in the Nations—lost men with lost souls looking for something they were never going to find, especially peace and prosperity. They'd been better off being half-bloods like Cherokee Bill and Henry Starr than full-blooded skins.

"Sorry, can't do you no good. Now stand aside."

They stood for a moment longer then stepped aside. He'd seen no firearms on them and so was not worried, but to make sure he'd left the flap of his coat open long enough they could see the revolver riding his hip.

"Shit . . ." he heard one of them say.

Later, after the other members of the gang departed, the Indians returned and slaughtered the barkeep with a hatchet and emptied the cash register. And for added measure, they slit his throat with a bone-handled knife. It was later reported in the newspaper that the bloodletters had been part of a group of youths who called themselves the Rufus Buck gang and that their leader was a stone-faced young killer named Mamoa July.

Their song of death dangling from the end of the hangman's ropes had not yet been sung, but it would.

Chapter 13

You might not say I was lucky to get shot in the foot, but I was. You see while I was semi–laid up healing from a drunk's bullet wound, I met Mattie Mowbry. A schoolteacher there in Tulsa where the footshot doctors were. I met her at a pie dance, even though I could not dance very well considering the circumstances—felt like I was stepping on coals every time I tried to shake a leg. She took pity on me, I guess it was, for she came over with a cup of punch and said, "Looks like you could use a drink, cowboy. Horse step on you?"

"No ma'am, I got tangled up with the wrong cuss."

"Wasn't a woman, I hope," she said.

Said it with a wink, her russet hair bunched atop her head and cute as a button. 'Bout knocked my socks off, a woman like that being so game and bold as to make the first move.

We found a place to sit and talk while the music played and before either of us knew it, the hours fled and the whole shebang closed down for the night. The musicians packed up their instruments and the folks all drifted into the night.

I had a rig parked outside and I drove her home and told her I'd like to see her again and she said she'd like that too.

It wasn't but a month went by and we got hitched in her hometown in Arkansas City, Kansas, her folks looking on. Leastways I was healed enough then to limp down the aisle with but a cane to aid me.

I told her that night, "I know now what true love is."

"I think it was fate that brought us together, Heck," she said. "But please promise me not to let yourself get shot again."

"I promise," I told her.

Then she said as we were getting ready for the matrimonial bed, "Do you want more children, Heck? I know you're hurting over the ones you have but can't see very often?"

"Yes, Mattie, I want more children—with you. Children are the angels of the earth."

We blew out the lights and got started on the task at hand.

I dreamt the other night in silence of winter's snowfall, that a sweet, sweet woman knocked on my door and I opened it and there she stood glowing like some sort of angel come to earth—Mattie Mowbry, now Mattie Thomas.

We sat before the fire sharing coffee in tin cups laced with bourbon whiskey and she spoke of a place with healing waters she said would cure both a man's broken bones and his spirit.

I tell you what, when I awakened and saw it was a dream, I damn near wept.

I was lying in a cold empty room, my new wife and first child with her clear over in Tulsa while I was once more seeking out miscreants and nothing but bleakness all about me there in Lawton, in the small cabin of a friend who'd lent it to me while I was in town.

To add to my disappointment, the visitor at the door was not my Mattie, but Bill Tilghman who came trudging up through the snow, his rubber boots squeaking and buckles jingling. He stood stamping his cold feet there on the little bitty porch knocking loose the snow then ducked in under the lintel trying not to get a eye put out by hanging icicles. He was dressed in a duck coat and canvas britches and said, "But goddamn ain't it cold?"

Shut the door behind him and said, "You got coffee on yet?"

"Not yet, but I'm fixing to fire up a pot if you can tolerate the wait."

"I can tolerate almost any damn thing there is but frozen feet," he chimed and took off his beaver hat and hung it on the knob of a

kitchen chair and sat himself down.

I made the coffee and he said, "That the best you have, Arbuckle? I sorta prefer that new brand, Maxwell House, me and Zoe do. You tried it yet?"

"I'm good with Arbuckle," I said and he sort of looked momentarily glum and I said, "Well, maybe you ought to head on home again and get Zoe to fix you some of that Maxwell House." Mornings weren't my best time for being of a friendly nature and Bill was always putting the needle in me anyway simply because he enjoyed it. I guess he figured if he made other people miserable with his needling he wouldn't feel so miserable himself.

"Been another bad killing," he said sitting there, his one leg crossed over the other, waggling his foot impatiently for the coffee to get done percolating.

"Hell, I ain't surprised," I said. "You want some breakfast?"

"Yeah, I could stand to eat me something. It's a long damn cold ride over here. I started out way before daylight and Zoe was still asleep. Didn't want to disturb her."

"Who was it got killed?" I said, slicing slab bacon into a heavy black fry pan before getting some eggs from the wire basket.

"Bartender over in Ingalls."

"Who was it killed him, they know yet? Was it any of the Doolin gang?"

"No, this time it wasn't them. It was a bunch of Creeks and some of them nigger kids. Call themselves the Rufus Buck gang after their leader. Witnesses said there wasn't a one looked over seventeen years old. Just went in and murdered the poor fellow for his cash drawer money and a case of bonded whiskey."

He studied his hat like he didn't recognize it.

"Kids with guns," he said disgustedly. "What the hell is this old world coming to?"

"Shit, what's new?" I said, still half asleep, still thinking about my sweet wife who moments before had been consorting with me in the

most blissful nature you could imagine and promises in her eyes.

"I reckon the entire country's gone crazed with bloodletting," Bill said as I poured him a coffee of Arbuckle and watched him staring at it the way he had done with his hat, his own haughty image in the wet black mirror in his cup staring back at him.

"Speaking of which, you getting any closer to making an arrest of Arkansas Tom Jones?" he said.

"Got word he's in the area, but so far he's well hid out, but I'll get him."

"He's probably praying you won't, being from a preaching family like he is," Bill said with more than just a touch of irony and humor. "It would shame his folks to pieces he was to be arrested."

"You want sugar, some of this canned milk in it?"

"No," he said. "But I'll take a few of them eggs to go with that fatback, though, if you don't mind."

"Why don't I just tie on an apron and me and you get married," I said sarcastically.

"That's a damn fine idea, Heck, except I'm already married and so are you. Speaking of which, how's that new wife working out for you?"

"She's better than I deserve," I said.

"Oh, I'd say she's done all right for herself," he said as I fried up the eggs and bacon. "Sometimes you sell yourself too short, Heck."

"No use to butter me up, I'm already frying your eggs."

He laughed at that, said, "They hatcheted that barkeep and cut his throat too . . ."

I shook my head in wonderment at the potential for man's cruelty.

"How's the foot?" he said.

"Foot's fine, except when it gets cold or a rain's bound to come, then it aches like a bad tooth."

He sighed and took out his pipe and filled it with tobacco from a leather pouch then struck a match with his thumbnail and held it to the bowl, smoked and sipped his coffee while the bacon sizzled and popped.

"Men like us," he said, but never finished his thought. Just got lost in his thinking like he had a tendency to do. He was a good man, Bill Tilghman was. As good a man as ever I knew.

I fished eggs and bacon onto plates and set one before him then sat down myself and we ate like two men getting ready to go to work on the railroad.

Bill had done about everything you could think of in his lifetime. He'd been a buffalo hunter—claimed he'd killed more than ten thousand of them—had gone into the saloon business in Dodge City even though he hardly ever drank, was a deputy sheriff there in Dodge City too. Worked for Bat Masterson. And by the time I met him he was, like myself, a United States deputy marshal.

We hit it right off as friends, me and him and the big Dane Chris Madsen. Seemed like our fates would forever be tied long as we wore the badge in this wild and awful and wonderful territory.

Bill finished his eggs and bacon, wiping up the plate with half a cold biscuit left over from the day before and washing the last bite down with the coffee.

"You ain't a half-bad cook," he said.

"You want more?" I said.

"No, I'm good. 'Sides, I got to get on to Ingalls in time for supper."

He stood from the table and fixed his hat on his head and took out his watch to check the hour then snapped the lid closed and slipped it back into the pocket of his waistcoat.

"You need some money?" he said. "I'm flush."

Bill probably collected more reward money than me and Chris put together. He was hell on wheels running down miscreants with rewards on their heads. Said it gave him double pleasure: arresting the bad actors and getting paid reward money to do it.

"No. I'm set," I said.

"Well, hell, I just figured you being a newlywed and all, you'd

want to buy Mattie a dress or something to send to her, let her know you miss her." He winked in that mischievous way he had and added: "Maybe some silk bloomers for when you get home."

"Lord God," I said. "Ain't nothing sacred with you."

He just smiled slantwise and went on out into the air.

He buttoned his coat and turned up the collar then tugged on his riding gloves as he stood there breathing in all that cold brittle sky.

"Why if it wasn't so damn beautiful, all this snow," he said, "it'd make a man suicidal. Someday I get ahead enough I'm thinking about going where there is palm trees and a big ol' ocean to swim in. California maybe."

He stepped off the porch into snow up past his boot ankles then mounted his stud horse and turned its head out toward the road to Ingalls and rode off like a man without a care in the world.

I called out to him just before he got out of earshot: "Why you going all the way to Ingalls for lunch, Bill?" already knowing the answer.

"Maybe see can I get a line on the whereabouts of that so-called gang of ruffians," he called, half turning in his saddle. "There's already a reward of five hundred dollars on them. A hundred for each of their miserable little heads."

He waved a hand and rode off into the whiteness of the deepest time of winter. I did have to admit to myself that it was a righteous sight, all that snow making everything look pure and for once without evil—the frosted trees, the white shapes of things, the sky so blue that it looked like a dream of winter.

I went back inside and sat at the table and had myself another cup of coffee and then got down paper and pen and started writing a letter to Mattie, pouring out my love and lonesomeness to her. With her I could share my most private thoughts, and did.

When I finished the letter, I dressed and shaved my face and put the letter in the pocket of my sheephide coat, then went out and saddled my horse and rode to town to mail it.

I sure hoped I'd catch Arkansas Tom Jones soon so I could go home for a spell before the next job came along.

Damn his sorry hide, anyway.

CHAPTER 14

Like denned bears they were aroused by the symphony of spring, the drip of melting ice, the shrinking of snow under warming sun, the gurgle of creeks flowing once more, the ache of weathered boards expanding in new heat.

"What's that?" said Newcomb to his unholy bride, the girl child Rose Dunn.

She listened in the bed next to him, pale-skinned and thin-boned like a young stork, eyes as black and shiny as wet stones.

"What, George? I don't hear nothing."

"Why, listen to it," he said, sitting up on the side of the bed to tug on his boots and then rising and clumping to the window, his pale bare haunches like a pair of unleavened bread loaves. The light was like polished silver.

"It's water dripping," he said over his shoulder.

Rose seemed confused.

"Ain't you ever heard dripping water before, George?"

"Why sure I have. But do you know what it means?"

"It's something that's leaked?" she said with all innocence. She was not by nature a very bright girl, but her slattern beauty made up for her mental shortcomings.

"No," he said, peering out the window. "It means spring has finally arrived. Why the sun is melting the snow and the icicles on the eaves. By God! Us boys can get back to business again. The damn winter is no more!"

He whooped and did a little jig, his boots knocking the

floorboards.

"Why you're as silly as a goose," she giggled at the sight of a fully naked man dancing about in just his boots.

"How 'bout fixing us some breakfast grub?" he said, sitting down on the bed again to tug off his boots and put on his trousers before tugging his boots back on again.

Looking at him like that, bent over, his broad back exposed, she said, "We might be the whitest people in the territory, George, what with all the Injuns and niggers about."

He laughs, said, "That damn Tulsa Blake is whiter than me."

"My brothers are all darker than me," Rose said, her lips pursed in wonderment.

"Maybe your pap is got some Creek blood in him," Newcomb said teasingly.

Rose had to think about that a moment, for she could barely remember what her pa looked like, he'd been gone from her life for so long.

"Maybe," she said. "Pap was always a mystery to me."

George watched her dress. He liked watching her in all her various stages of dress and undress.

"You're as sweet as a can of peaches," he said, "and I'd love you even if you was some Injun or nigger, either."

She felt in a way blessed to have such a man care for her the way the much older Newcomb did. Most gals her age had beaus who were mere boys, and not hardcases with reputations like George Bitter Creek Newcomb, not as manly as he. She knew that her brothers, some of them, weren't overly fond of her being with him, that sometimes they seemed even jealous. But she could care less. Happiness, after all, was in such short supply in hardship land. Besides, George was sort of like a lover and a pa all wrapped into one.

Roy Daugherty went by the name Arkansas Tom Jones because it sounded bolder. He carried a Yellow Boy Henry repeating rifle because it's flashier than your ordinary Winchester. He wore Mexican spurs because they jingled louder than the smaller rowel spurs of the ordinary cowman. He wore a black hat and a black cowhide vest and walked with a swagger as if he's ready to punch the world in the mouth. Everywhere he went he had bad intentions and flinty hard eyes. He was unafraid of life and even less afraid of death. Everything about this world seemed to him a cruel hoax. It's a moment-by-moment existence, like breathing.

Why let a man be born and learn the pleasures of sin if'n all you're going to do is grow old and die? he often wondered. "It seems to me like some bad joke played on us by him," he will say aloud at times even if nobody was listening. The Mexican mustang lineament put him half out of his head crazy.

Of course, few who might witness and listen to his rambling tirades understand him, for they come and go like prairie winds and his angst was not singular but multiplied by almost everything, authority most especially: the government, the laws, the very forces of nature, a sore hip, and unfaithful women.

He would, at times, sit for hours watching traffic on the streets of Ingalls as if watching for something or someone in particular when in fact he's merely idling away the hours for lack of anything better to do. He was a man without foresight, a waiter of events he himself was incapable of conjuring up.

He had a sweetheart in Eufaula, a plain woman his ma's age, who treated him with a certain mothering jealousy, and sometimes he craved being with her and other times he couldn't stand the thought.

He leaned and spit into the cold dirt, his fists balled into the pockets of his coat.

"Boy I sure do hate this old world sometimes," he told himself.

And yet, he had a growing feeling of expectancy, that

something large will happen one day, something that will change how things are and that life will be different and no longer will he be bored to death.

Her name was Kate Thornbush, the woman in Eufaula. He saw her when her husband was away. She had a son about his age, a boy named Elbert, an opium addict presently locked up in the county jail for theft. Last time he was there, she complained and wept as he shucked out of his clothes, saying: "Elbert, Elbert, what am I going to for my darling boy?"

He offered no sympathy.

"Come crawl in this bed with me," he ordered, "before your husband comes home."

They fornicated and drank absinthe she called the Green Fairy. Tom had never experienced anything quite like it, said to her, "Hell I might just become a dope fiend myself." Ignored the bitter sting of his comments upon her pinched face.

His habit was to stay with her a day or two or three and then ride out before her husband returned, and all the while, when not fornicating or drinking the green liquor, she would cry about Elbert and blame herself for his condition.

And though the very heart of winter had passed into memory, the spring wind was cold and lashing as whips against bare skin.

Someone came along and called him by name, a man in a gray hat. "Howdy, Tom. Don't reckon you'd buy a feller a drink?"

He eyed the fellow.

"Shit, why not?"

Soon enough, he thought that he'll ride off and find Doolin and see about getting on with his bunch. It'd be something to do, at least. Beat the hell out of just sitting around drinking with rummies.

"Listen to that goddamn wind blow," the fellow said, lifting his glass.

The air inside the saloon was fetid and smoky dim with cigar smoke and the sickly sweetness of full spittoons and the sweat of sweaty whores and the pomade of a pimp's slicked-back hair and sawdust on the floor.

"Shit," he said. "I guess."

The fellow he was drinking with blinked. Didn't know what to say. Not even "thank you."

Tom tossed back his drink, thought briefly of the woman in Eufaula, crying, "Oh, Elbert. Oh, Elbert!" and it put a knot in his stomach.

How easy it was she spread her legs for him. *A woman never forgets how,* he thought. *They never goddamn do. If it was just that easy for a man,* he thought.

Chapter 15

It is the big Dane Chris Madsen this time who came to visit, to deliver the news that Henry Starr shot and killed a deputy U.S. marshal over in Lenapah Indian Territory.

Said, "You know Floyd Wilson, the deputy got shot?"

I said no. "Me either," he said.

"They get Starr?"

"Got him in the jailhouse."

"That whole Starr clan is nothing but trouble. Always was, always will be."

"Amen to that."

We listened to the raucous winter wind. It howled like mourning women at a funeral of their children, like the widows of good lawmen killed over nothing but trying to do their job. Only thing that stood between the honest world and total anarchy was us.

The big Dane seemed to take up the whole room. Mattie served us coffee then went and attended to the baby who learned to squall pretty damn good for someone so small.

"Marriage looks like it's been good for you, Heck," Chris said above the babe's protestations.

"With the right woman it is," I said.

"Amen to that."

Mattie soothed the baby by putting it to her breast. I heard the familiar sound of the little one's suckling in the other room. If Chris heard it too he didn't let on.

"You know Heck," he said. "Speaking of them Starrs, there's one

crime that still troubles me to this day: who it was blew ol' Belle Starr out from under her feather hat at point-blank range, both barrels. They say you couldn't even recognize her the way some of that buckshot tore up her face."

"Why that's been what, two, three years ago. Why concern yourself with it, Dane?"

Chris shook his head. He put on bulk since the last we met, or as he liked to call it, winter fat, like some old denned-up bear.

"Well, of all the crimes committed in the territory, you'd a thought somebody would have stepped up and claimed the murder, or somebody spill the beans. Belle had about as many enemies as she had lovers."

"I'd reckon if she'd had reward money on her head, ol' Bill Tilghman might have gone and dug her up for it and claimed he did it."

Chris laughed that big booming laugh of his and I had to caution him to keep it down so as not to disturb the child who was now silent and probably asleep with a belly full of warm mother's milk.

"I do have to say that Belle was one butt-ugly woman," he sniggered. "I doubt them buckshot did anything to steal her beauty."

We both propped up our socked feet on ottomans, used to dark humor, for it was a way to get past some of the pitiful ugly things we'd seen as lawmen.

"How you reckon it was she got all those men attracted to her, being homely as a horse? First it was Cole Younger's uncle she married, then she took up with the likes of that bootlegger Sam Starr. And after Sam was killed in that shootout with ol' Frank West, Belle ended up with a whole series of men in her bed. It was like she was just all sugar tit when it came to men."

He shook his head in disbelief.

"Yes," I said, reeling off the names of some of the others Belle had conjugated with: Jack Spaniard, Jim French, and the bloodluster Blue Duck, in most recent memory. There were probably a lot more than any of us knew about.

"Maybe she paid them," Chris opined.

"She would have me," I said and he grinned more.

"She sure as hell was rough on men, as many of 'em that ended up dead or in prison," Chris said.

We raised our glasses and Chris said, "Here's to justice and may the damned be damned again."

"Amen."

For a while we listened to sleet pelt the window glass and the wind rattle the door and Chris looked about and said, "I bet it feels good to have family in this house again."

"Feels heaven sent."

"What would men like us do without a good woman behind us?" he said.

It was my belief that we both felt that somewhere beneath the warmth of fires and good coffee and warm beds, and even loving wives, that everything was so temporary, that our lives and those of our loved ones could be snatched away in an instant. The lives of lawmen especially in these treacherous times were most precarious. To quote Mr. Shakespeare's Hamlet, *"We knew that murder was most foul." A bullet don't ever stop and ask who's firing it and who's it aimed for.*

It was rough country. Rough as a cob in so many ways. Winters will freeze you and summers burn you. And in between you have tornados, floods, droughts, and fires.

"Come the spring," Chris said after a moment of studying his face in his cup, "we'll be back at it, Heck. The rats will come out of their holes and the carnage will begin anew."

"I know it," I said without enthusiasm as I thought of wife and child in the other room.

"Maybe we're getting too old to keep at this kind of work," he said forlornly.

"Maybe. But if not us, who will do it?"

"There's plenty of others, younger men than us, Heck."

"Well, what would we do, Chris, me and you and Bill Tilghman? Sit around and play checkers?"

He contemplated on it for a few moments, then leaned forward and said in a conspiratorial tone, "I don't suppose you'd have a dollop of popskull to go in this coffee, would you?"

"You know, I just might," I said. "I lay in extra for when you and them others come round. Now if I just had more friends like Tilghman, I'd save a ton on liquor supplies alone."

"And here he run himself a saloon once't and don't even drink. Why that just ain't right, Heck."

I rose up out of my chair and went into the kitchen, reached up in the cupboard, and got down a bottle I kept for things such as snakebite and to rub on the baby's gums when it got fussy. Cutting teeth will make a baby fussy. I poured a thimbleful in mine and Chris's cup and he took to it like a kid with Christmas candy. It's a joy to see good friends enjoying themselves.

"That's right fair," he said, tasting it. "Where'd you get it?"

"I confiscated it off a whiskey peddler back in the early spring. Had a whole case. I had to, of course, test it to make sure it was the real thing and not commit no false arrest."

"Well, if you ever arrest him again, get some over my way, 'cause it don't ever hurt to get a second opinion."

We sat and enjoyed some of these fruits of our labor till Chris blinked like some old turtle and said, "You know, I almost can't wait for spring to get here so we can get on the chase again. Clean out these vipers once and for all. Why it won't be too much longer and it will be a whole new century. Ain't that something, getting to live in two centuries?"

"I'd feel a bit more charmed by the idea if and when it gets here," I said. "We both know how it is when you're chasing a man with a loaded gun and no need to get caught."

"True enough. But we live us charmed lives, Heck."

I spilled a tad more into our cups and we sipped until I heard Mattie in the other room, the runners on the rocking chair just like two regular fellows.

After a time more Chris rose up and said, "Well, I can't do no more good round here. I have any more of this hooch and I'll be spilling out of my saddle and what will the church goers think of me then?"

I walked outside with him and watched him ride off then rejoined my wife there on the divan where she was paging through a McCall's *magazine.*

"The baby sleeping?"

"Yes, the dear thing," she said.

"It's been a good day so far, what with a visit from old friends, a beautiful wife and young'n taking up space in this ol' house again."

"It has," she says.

I drew her near and kissed her cheek.

"Is that the best you got?" she said with a devilish grin.

"Why? What you have in mind, woman?"

It was not yet noon. It didn't seem to matter. She took my hand and led me to the bedroom.

Yes, everything in the outer world will just have to wait a bit longer.

Book II

Ingalls, O.T., 1893

The Death Trap

The outlaw business had fared well throughout the spring and summer of 1893, and the boys as usual—Doolin, Red Buck Weightman, Bitter Creek, Tulsa Jack, Dynamite Dick, Charlie Pierce, Bill Dalton, and Arkansas Tom Jones—had once more taken their refuge in Ingalls where as usual they holed up in rooms at the OK Hotel passing their days in pleasure of card playing, whiskey drinking, lie swapping, retelling of tales of adventure and misfortune, and of course the saloon girls next door at Ransom's Saloon.

These were their glory days, Doolin told them more than once.

"We'll never again know such times as these," he shouted above the din in the saloon. It was near midnight and things had the feel of just getting started. So far nobody had shot, stabbed, or punched anybody else, but the air had that expectancy to it.

It wasn't just the boys who occupied Ransom's. There were assorted punchers and teamsters, pimps, pool hall hustlers, and a one-eyed piano player thrown into the mixture. Behind the bar four keeps kept busy pouring iced beer and mixing cocktails. Between the raised level of conversation, hammered piano keys, glass clinking, shrill laughter of the demimondes, curses, and clack of billiard balls, a man could hardly hear himself think.

But thinking never was much the order of business in such waning and waxing hours.

Dynamite Dick Clifton and Bitter Creek Newcomb were shooting a game of billiards with a couple of saloon chippies, a pair of sisters from New Rumley, Ohio, where the now most famous dead soldier in the country—George Armstrong Custer—had been born. The names of the sisters were Agnes and Lillie Belle Bushroot. The boys sniggered every time one of the chippies took a shot. They couldn't play pool worth a damn, but it didn't matter.

Red Buck Weightman had himself his own chippie in one of the back rooms and she kept insisting that he remove his boots so as not to filthy up the sheets and he kept insisting whatever business they were about to conduct would not take long enough to make it worth his while to remove his footwear. Still, she insisted.

"You never know when I might need to make a run for it," Red argued. "A man with the laws always on his trail has got to always be on caution."

But the chippy stood firm and Red finally relented, cursing under his breath the whole time. And when he'd gotten his boots off, the chippy said, "Lord, I wished now I'd let you kept them on. You ever wash you feet?"

Bill Dalton was his usual taciturn self, sitting alone, silent with a brooding visage. He was yet aggrieved over the death of his brothers almost a year previous in Coffeyville. His tetchy manner made it such that nobody much cared to share his company, which suited him fine.

Charlie Pierce, Tulsa Jack, and Doolin sat at a table playing stud poker, Tulsa Jack looking all the tough with the stub of an unlit cigar poking from the corner of his grizzled mouth. His humorless feral eyes studied yet another losing hand: two trays, a six of hearts, a seven of diamonds, and a ten of spades. His luck had been running dumb all evening.

Arkansas Tom, a tall, slender individual with different-colored eyes—brown and blue—had taken to a sickbed in the upper story of the hotel. He suffered from a chest cold and fever. He didn't have the strength of a ten-year-old. There wasn't any medico in the burg, so he paid a chippie to help nurse himself with a bottle of whiskey and a deck of playing cards that had images of naked dancing Cyprians wrapped in sheer scarves. The chippie was bucktooth and seemed as titillated by the images as was Tom.

Tulsa Jack folded.

Doolin raked in the pot, a total of twenty dollars, all of it stolen money from an express railroad car a month previous over near Red River. They were hounded by the locals in a running chase and twice they lost the posses before the locals decided they were dealing with better men than themselves.

Recent word came down that a new man had been installed by Judge Parker to bring the gang to bay, a Marshal E.D. Nix.

"You ever heard of him?" Doolin asked members of the gang more than once in their fragmentary conversations.

They shook their heads.

"He's like them others," Tulsa Jack said, "he'll be hellbent for the reward on our heads."

"Shit can't blame 'em for that," Charlie Pierce said with a grin. "Man's gotta make a living, same as us."

"Stacking up corpses is as good as any way to do it," Jack said back.

"You boys sure do know how to bring down rain on a man's parade," Doolin said sourly. For months now he'd been dogged with a dark premonition that he would not live much longer. It sometimes felt like he was trying to race a train to the crossing and his horse half lame.

When the laws came, Arkansas Tom lay abed, the chippie gone off somewhere, the cards untouched atop the small nightstand. The fevered dreams had him locked in a cycle of sameness, like being trapped in quicksand to where the more he struggled to break free, the more it held him.

In one of the dreams, he was being molested by a hired man on his pap's farm, when Tom was hardly yet come into his manhood.

Tom was trying to fend him off with a pitchfork, but the fellow had bolted the barn doors and was pursuing him up the haymow ladder. He awakened twice screaming into the empty room, no one to hear, no one to attend him.

The laws entered the town with all due caution, rifles at the ready. They were United States deputy marshals and a few Indian police.

Word had reached the ears of Marshal E.D. Nix that the Doolin gang was holed up in Ingalls, had been for the better part of a week. Nix aimed to end their fun and assigned his best man, Deputy John Hixon, to lead the posse.

"You be wary of that bunch," Nix warned. "They won't go easy and you shouldn't give them any quarter."

"We got enough to handle 'em." Hixon was confident in the abilities of the heavily mustachioed lawman, less so in the Indian police who were to join them. "It's time we rid the country of such vermin."

"Well, capture what many of them you can."

"Otherwise?"

"Bury 'em good and deep."

Hixon nodded.

★ ★ ★ ★ ★

Up from the creek where they'd camped during that long raucous night they approached the little nothing of a town at first light, each man jack of them knowing the reputation of what the newspapers had come to call the *Oklahombres.*

From outward appearances, it might as well have been a slow procession of saddle tramps, down-on-their-luck drifters simply looking for a place to get a beer while asking about work locally.

Most in Ingalls were yet asleep that hour of the morning, the first dawn sky the color of cheap gray paint.

The blacksmith was up at that hour stoking the coal fire for his forge and he saw them. He had thick arms and wore a leather apron. A drover headed back to some far-flung ranch with a heavy head of whiskey vapors and pockets that had been full of a month's pay when he rode in but were now flat as Hattie's flapjacks. A boy with an ungainly limp just coming to town from his pa's hardscrabble place to wait at the drugstore for it to open so he could buy a bottle of cough syrup for his sickly ma noticed them too. He stared until one of them glanced his way then averted his eyes.

The lawmen's horses plodded purposefully; nobody seemed to be in any hurry. Hixon had ordered that they seem casual hoping to take the outlaws by surprise, hence the early hour.

"The miscreants will no doubt be asleep," Hixon said. "Men like them tend to be revelers."

There was an eeriness to it: the slow, steady clop of hooves on the hardpan, the jangle of bits, the breathless air. Too perfect of a morning it seemed.

The boy waiting for the drugstore to open took them into account once more because of the armament the men sported, how they rode with the butts of their Winchesters resting on their thighs, the barrels pointed skyward. He wore one strap of his coveralls hitched over a freckled bare shoulder.

The fate of all the men that day, White and Red, good and bad, evil and perhaps less evil, was foretold—according to a preacher who would later on preach on the violence that day—ten thousand years ago, writ in the Book of Fates, scribbled by the hand of God.

And so it seemed.

It was a day that exploded with the suddenness of a thunderstorm.

It had begun as a morning like any other, and would end like no other.

One of the deputies, Dick Speed, was anxious to see justice done, had an itchy finger. He would be the first to fire a shot, the first to die as well.

In the Ransom Saloon, Doolin and the others were running down like unwound pocket watches with a minute left before they stopped ticking altogether. They had drank several bottles of liquor and played cards and chased the hurdy-gurdy girls with an all-night passion. Dynamite Dick had lost the rest of his pocket money in a game of billiards to Red Buck Weightman.

The last drop of liquor in the last bottle had been poured and swallowed.

Bitter Creek Newcomb was eager to return to the lusty young Rose and so bid adieu to his weary companions, some of whom had fallen asleep where they sat.

"I got to get on," he said, as though it mattered to anyone there, and headed for the door.

Doolin sat heavy-headed. He'd overdone it this time and he knew it. Like the others he had not denied himself any pleasure a man can find in a saloon and now felt a shade guilty because Edith called to him in the back of his mind.

"Shit," he muttered. Tulsa Jack opened his eyes.

"What'd you say, Bill?"

Just then the crack of gunfire outside. Sounded like a rifle. Close. They heard Bitter Creek shout a curse.

Dick Speed and the others had come to within a dozen yards of the saloon and dismounted their horses, levered shells into their Winchesters, and fanned out in their approach and were advancing when Bitter Creek came out the front door, eyes cast downward, and started to mount his horse. He'd gotten one foot in the stirrup when Dick Speed shot him.

The slug struck Bitter Creek in the hip and screwed him into the ground. He yelped like a whipped child. But his gunfighter instincts took over and he drew the big Russian Model Scholf .44, snapping off two, three, four shots. His aim was good. His aim was true. And Dick Speed was no more.

The other laws opened fire into the saloon. And just like that the amicable peace of sleepy Ingalls, Oklahoma Territory, was shattered, the first blood spilled.

Up in his sick room on the second floor of the hotel, Arkansas Tom came alert and ran to the window with his rifle in hand. He was dressed in just his long handles. He broke out the glass that overlooked the saloon and attached livery, took aim down on the gathered deputies.

Why shit, it'd be like shooting fish in a barrel. He was about to fire a round into Hixon but a running target caught his eye and he swung the barrel round and fired. He always did admire his abilities with a rife.

The kid who'd been standing in front of the drugstore waiting for it to open so he could buy his sickly ma a bottle of cough syrup had broken cover and ran like a spooked rabbit directly into Tom's front iron sights. The slug tore through him armpit to bowel and slammed him flat. He tried to speak, to cry for help, but could not. He knew he was dying, but still didn't believe it.

Murray the barkeep came out firing a shotgun and was immediately wounded by the deputies.

Arkansas Tom found another target and let Marshal Hueston have one of his slugs through the upper back and watched the lawman topple forward.

By the time the others inside ran out the front door of the saloon to the attached open stable where they'd tied their horses, the air was a cloud of gunsmoke. The gunfire crackled back and forth like so much electricity. Everyone with a gun was frenzied, it was kill or be killed.

Most of the boys made their horses and helped the wounded Bitter Creek make his even as blood from his hip wound soaked his trouser leg and filled his boot.

Bill Dalton, in the lead, mounted his horse and started to ride out but deputy Lafayette Shadley fired on him, missed the rider but killed the horse, spilling Dalton to the dirt. Tulsa Blake, or maybe it was Charlie Pierce, ran up and offered a hand and swung Dalton aboard behind them. Doolin turned and shot Shadley just as he was levering another shell. The wound was not instantly mortal, but the deputy knew instinctively he was a goner. Dying men know things that living men do not.

Dynamite Dick and Charlie Pierce both felt the sting of bullets but it didn't stop them from running from the field of battle.

In minutes there was only one outlaw left in the town of Ingalls.

Hixon called for Tom to come out hands in the air.

"I ain't coming!" Tom shouted down, his voice still weak from his recent illness. "You boys will air me out."

"We won't air you," Hixon promised.

"Shit, when'd I ever believe what the law had to say?"

"Your choice!" Hixon called then told one of the deputies to throw a stick of dynamite into the hotel.

"Thought E.D. wanted us to bring 'em in alive?"

"Not my decision to make," he said, pointing with his chin to the upper room. "It's his."

"Oh."

The deputy went and got a stick of dynamite.

"Last chance," Hixon called up to Tom.

Tom answered with a rifle shot that rang on the blacksmith's anvil, the blacksmith cursing, "You son of a bitch."

The deputy came with the dynamite.

"Light her and toss her in," Hixon ordered.

They waited for the explosion.

When it came the windows of the hotel all shattered and the building itself trembled.

"All right, all right! I'm coming out, don't shoot me, boys!"

Hixon looked at the remaining deputies, but there was no joy on his face—the dead and wounded were too many, the bulk of the miscreants fled. It was a bust.

"Damn it to hell," he muttered to no one. "Damn it to hell."

I knew those boys Doolin's bunch killed over in Ingalls. It was stunning news. Not only had three lawmen been slaughtered, but the only one of Doolin's bunch to be captured was Roy Daugherty, alias Arkansas Tom Jones. Said they had to use dynamite to smoke him out. Said he had the look of a man who'd been hit with a sledge hammer. Too bad the dynamite didn't do the trick on him.

I went on up to the prison in Lansing, Kansas, to look in on him. I just had to see with my own eyes what this hardcase looked like.

I was surprised; he looked timid as a schoolteacher. Couldn't have weighed more than one hundred and forty pounds with rocks in his pockets. Soft-spoken. Polite. Lean as a beanpole.

"So you're him?" I said.

"Yes, sir, reckon I am."

He sat across from me, manacled wrist and ankle. A guard in a gray suit with a sawed-off shotgun stood by the heavy steel door. All through the halls of that heinous place you could hear catcalls echoing off the stonework, the sounds of desperate men. Damn place looked like some medieval fortress, and I guess it was.

"They gave me fifty years," he said softly, as though offended like he'd been treated unfairly.

"I reckon you should count your blessings they didn't drop you through a hangman's trap on that big gallows outside," I said.

He merely smiled the way a kid would who'd gotten away with stealing a warm pie off some woman's windowsill.

"Was my folks and people who got them to have sympathy on me," he said. "I come from a long line of preachers. Pa, brothers, two uncles."

"Guess it didn't take hold with you, then, all that religion—thou shall not murder and such?"

He nodded.

"Guess not," he said.

"Where the rest of those boys hiding out these days?" I asked.

He shrugged. "Here, there, everywhere, I reckon."

"Might be able to help you some you tell me where they're holed up?"

He shrugged again.

"I came here to find out where Doolin and them is, to look into the eyes of a murderous son of a bitch."

He grinned slowly until a row of sharp teeth emerged, one of the front ones laid over the other.

"I reckon you're crazier than a fevered coon."

I left out of that front gate and didn't look back. I knew one thing: maybe spending fifty years inside that stone hell hole was a whole lot harder than being dropped through a hangman's trap.

At least for me it would be.

I called a meeting with the big Dane and Bill Tilghman and some of the others who were on Doolin's trail.

We swore to redouble our efforts, but knowing no matter what we did, unless we caught a lucky break and got an informant to come forth, that bunch of miscreants could be anywhere in three states. It was mighty big and spread-out country.

The night I visited Arkansas Tom I lay in bed next to my wife, wide awake at midnight still and wondered if it was all worth it, chasing down men who were like ghosts, learning of good friends' deaths at the hands of that wild bunch. Seemed like the only ones with luck on their side was them, not us.

I didn't fall asleep until it was time to get up.

My nerves all jangled.

I wanted them and I wanted them bad. We all felt the same, some saying we should simply kill them where we found them, and others opting to follow the law and arrest them and see them to a fair trial.

I wasn't sure at all which side I came down on anymore. Tom Hueston had been a good friend of mine and now he was under the ground with a widow and kids sobbing over him.

Anger and the need for revenge clouds a man's judgment.

One of our boys said—I won't name him—we should just kill them all and let Jesus sort them out. To which there came several "Amens."

I drank my breakfast coffee, ate my eggs and bacon, and rode out once more; the name Bill Doolin printed on my mind like some article in the Police Gazette.

Chapter 16

The boys delivered the hip-shot Bitter Creek to his inamorata, Rose Dunn. The woman child wept when she saw how bloody he was, cried out loudly, "Don't leave me, Bill!"

"She does have a flair for the dramatic, don't she Bill?" Tulsa Blake said to Doolin, Blake himself nicked in a couple of places by almost fatal bullets, had been fortifying himself against the bitter pain with some of Doctor Haygood's Bitters, a concoction of woodgrain alcohol and opium.

Bitter Creek smiled grimly and said, "Shit, honey, it's just a bullet went through me is all it is. Ain't no laws ever gonna kill ol' Bitter Creek Newcomb."

Blake shook his head, said, "Looks like they both ought to join an acting troupe."

Doolin waited around while the other members of the gang scattered like hunted birds before the blast of pellets but vowing to meet up again once things cooled off.

"Cowboy Flats," Doolin had said. "About a month from now. Give us time to lick our wounds."

Doolin took a seat outside Newcomb's cabin while Rose went to work cleaning George's wounds, washing away the crusted blood and applying bandages she made from strips of torn underthings.

Doolin fashioned and smoked a cigarette and went over the Ingalls flight in his head again, how it was they were caught by surprise and nearly wiped out. Only way he could conclude it was that maybe there was a Judas among them. From one of the other nearby cabins three of the Dunn brothers strode forth looking dusty, slack-jawed, and mean-eyed. Their usual visage. They had the air of cur dogs in search of meat bones.

"Looks like you boys run into a buzz saw," Bee Dunn said when he came to stand in front of Doolin. Calvin and Dal looked on, thumbs hooked in the front pockets of their dungarees. Both wore sidearms, butts forward, right hip and left hip.

"Too bad they didn't finish that one in there," Dal said, nodding toward the cabin door.

"You don't like him any too much," Doolin said. "Why is that exactly?"

"It ain't nothing," Bee said. "Dal here's just a bit techy this time of morning, till he's had his grits and coffee don't you know."

Doolin didn't care for the Dunns—none of them, but Rose. He'd heard rumors it wasn't just stolen beef they dealt in their butcher shop, but also some bounty hunting too. Figured them to be back shooters. Killers for hire.

Dal looked at the door as if he was trying to see right through it.

"How bad he get it?" he said, his voice hopeful it was real bad.

"Might have knocked some bone off his hip, took a chunk of meat out of him, that's about all."

Dal's right eye twitched.

Bee was the cool one among them. Thing was, where were those other two brothers, the ones with him, Dal and Calvin, who always seemed a bit too twitchy.

Doolin casually eased his revolver out of its holster and held it in his lap.

"What's that supposed to mean?" Bee said.

"Nothing," Doolin said. "In case the laws were to suddenly come charging up."

Calvin and Dal looked around toward the road, too dumb to figure out why Doolin had taken out his pistol. Not Bee. He knew why.

"You don't have nothing to worry about from none of us," he said.

"I know it," Doolin said, but still did not put his gun back in the holster. Just held it there with one hand while he smoked his cigarette as casual as if he were waiting for the train to come in.

"You ain't gone make no friends around here acting that away," Bee warned.

"Wasn't aiming to," Doolin said.

He knew if anyone tried anything of the three it would probably be Dal first, the surly one. Surly and dumb were a bad combination.

They all stood around a moment longer then Bee said, "We got to get on to the butcher shop and help Bill and them out."

Doolin didn't say anything. No need to comment. Watched the Dunn brothers stride off toward the corral and rope and saddle their horses then ride off. He put his gun back in the holster.

They remained three or four days at the Dunn place, Doolin sleeping on the porch, sleeping light, listening for footsteps or hooves or anything at all that might approach.

He could hear inside the cabin, there in the dark, Bitter Creek and Rose going at it, Bitter Creek whimpering in pain, "Jesus, Rose honey, it ain't so easy doing it with this bum hip . . ."

"Oh Georgy, I'm sorry, baby. Rose will kiss it and make it all better."

"Pour me some more of that forty rod."

Doolin wished he had something to stopper his ears with.

Day four Doolin asked George if he was up to watching himself, that he wanted to get back to Edith for a couple of weeks before they all met again at Cowboy Flats.

"You probably heard us in there the other night," George said.

"I heard you in there every night," Doolin said.

"Shit, I reckon I'm up to standing watch for the laws," he said, hefting his Winchester. Rose had gone to the privy.

"It's not just the laws you ought to keep watch for," Doolin said.

"Why, what's up?"

"Those brothers of hers."

"Bee and them? Why I'm practically kin to them. What'd they want to do me harm for?"

"For one thing you're screwing their sister and I got the feeling some of them aren't too thrilled about it. For another, once those boys hear there's enough reward money on your head—and there might be now after Ingalls—they're just liable to lay you low and collect."

Bitter Creek's face formed into a mask of disappointment. Disappointment he was not more respected and thought kindly of. Disappointment thinking one of Rose's brothers could be jealous of him and Rose.

"Ah . . ." he said.

"You do what you want," Doolin said, saddling his horse. "But was it me, I wouldn't trust any of them far as I could fling a cat."

Doolin rode off and Bitter Creek watched him go. He hobbled back inside and first thing he did was put one of his pistols under his pillow. That evening lying abed he said in the darkness, "Rose, honey, you ever diddle any of them brothers of yorn?"

"Why what sort of stupid thing is that to say to me?" She

acted highly offended, but Bitter Creek couldn't tell if she was truly, or not.

"Nothing, just something I thought could have happened. Some of 'em keeps a close eye on you and me and don't overly act too friendly, is all."

"Oh, George, you're just worried 'cause the laws nearly killed you. I bet you don't trust nobody or nothing now for a little while."

"Maybe," he said.

She touched him. He felt the invisible bird-like hand of hers snake under the covers and take hold of him.

"How's that feel?" she said.

"Feels good," he said.

"I knew it would," she said.

"You're right, it does."

She giggled.

He tried to act like everything was fine, and in spite of his concerns about her brothers, he stiffened in her hand. He just couldn't help himself with Rose. She was too much child, too much woman, and too, too much temptation.

She started to move her hand.

Well, if they come, I'll kill them, he told himself. With this pistol under my pillow.

"Don't stop doing that," he said.

"I won't," she said.

They had no visitors that night and Bill slept like a dead man.

Chapter 17

Eureka Springs

Bill said, "Come with me."

Edith asked, "Where to, Bill? Why, it's almost midnight."

"Just come along," he said gently.

"I'll have to dress first," she said.

"Not necessary," he said. "Just wear what you have on."

She giggled and said, "Bill, you're being foolish."

"I know," he said.

He took her by the hand and led her out into the night and down to the property's warm springs that, in Bill's mind at least, had powers to heal old wounds, including a foot wound he'd gotten in a shootout years before. He and Edith had traveled by train to Eureka Springs, Arkansas, to rest after several more holdups following the Ingalls debacle. They partook of the warm waters. They dined each evening in the Crescent Hotel's ornate restaurant, everything from thick steaks to terrapin soup. And afterward they'd stroll the streets while Bill smoked a fancy cigar that cost four bits.

They made love and laughed and Bill took her shopping for clothes, hats, shoes, whatever she wanted in the fashionable shops all up and down the curving streets. They took in the sights of the stately Victorian houses with their three stories and turrets and quarried stone structures. They took carriage rides and ate candied apples.

The money from robbing trains and banks had made him fat

and sassy as a well-fed cat.

Moon's light played on the shimmering dark waters as they reached the edge of the pool. "Shuck out of your clothes, honey," Bill said as he stripped off his coat, shirt, and trousers and stood naked before her.

"Oh, Bill," she said. "We're being wicked!" But said it with a tittering laugh.

He led her into the water until they were nearly shoulder deep, the warm silkiness twining around their bodies like loving caresses.

He reached for her with both hands and felt the sleekness of her body, slippery as a seal, and kissed her mouth long and deeply so that he became aroused and hefted her up so she could wrap her legs around his hips and he entered her, her body nearly weightless so that it was easy.

A gasp and it was begun. Her head tossed back, she saw the moon like a lost silver dollar somebody had dropped on black velvet.

She clung to him the whole while, wordless and happy as he moved into her, as he turned in a tight circle, holding her there impaled upon him. Each time she gasped and wordlessly he continued until he cried out in a sound that echoed in the dark.

He gently and slowly released her, like a prize fish he'd caught and was now giving back to the world from which he'd caught it. She floated away and he watched her, there on her back, her small breasts gleaming wet mounds above the water.

She called to him and he came to her and held her up like that, on her back, arms and legs floating on the surface.

"We are truly wicked," she said in a soft, happy voice.

"We are," he said.

"I love you, Bill Doolin."

"And I you, Edith Doolin."

Eventually they returned to their room.

"I'm thinking maybe we ought to go to New Mexico soon," he said. "A change of scenery might be good."

She was too tired and sleepy to listen or ask why New Mexico and before he knew it she was asleep. For once in a very long time he was truly happy and did not dream of murderous things.

For three weeks more they stayed on and bathed in the springs several times a day. They ate the finest meals and Bill dressed Edith like she was his queen. She was.

"Spending so much on such lavish things is a bit foolish, don't you think, Bill?"

He laughed off her concerns.

"The cattle business has been good lately," he said. "Real good."

They strolled along a tree-lined park and he smoked his fancy cigars and she tried her best not to be overly fretful at all the money they were spending, even though she quite enjoyed the lifestyle.

She'd never known such a man as Bill Doolin. All her previous beaus had been but boys, shy and often simple with simplistic plans for their lives: to become farmers, store clerks, ministers, barbers.

She had not been intimate with any of them, though there had been occasions where things got a bit frisky, where hands groped for certain pleasures—the young minister being the most randy of the lot, begging her, trying to claim it was God's wishes that they express their sexuality, or else, why would He have made them as they were?

"We are, Edith, you and I, all too human and with all too human needs . . ." the preacher's son chided, trying to take her hand and put it on him.

He tended to become whiny when he overly wanted something and she'd refused to keep seeing him.

Then one day into Stillwater had ridden this handsome bearded cowboy beneath a wide-brimmed Stetson looking like Jesus on a horse. He had those dark swarthy looks of a man long exposed to prairie winds and campfires and all the other elements of a cowboy's life.

He wore shotgun chaps and a leather vest over his striped shirt, a large blue kerchief like a dinner napkin draped around his throat.

It was his smile, though, that dazzled her, his smile and those ever-inquisitive dark brown eyes.

"Lord, you look like something God made," he said to her there in front of the mercantile as horsemen rode up and down the street, as children played hide-and-seek, as watchful eyes of men in front of the saloon looked on.

She blushed.

He doffed his wide-brimmed Stetson and slapped dust from it against his leg. His hair was dark and thick and longish. Never had she met or spoken to a man as handsome.

"My name's Bill," he said. "What's yours?"

She was so caught off guard that she told him.

"Edith," she blurted.

"That's a mighty fine name," he said. "Fits you."

Thing was, she knew he was overly trying to be charming, but the thing was too she didn't care.

"That's a real fine horse you've got, Bill."

She couldn't think of another thing to say to him, so discomfited as he'd made her.

He looked around at the horse, a tall, pie-bald mare.

"Oh, she ain't nothing special, Edith. Just a horse is all."

Now what? she wondered.

"Why we could go riding, if you'd like, Edith," he said.

Her father was inside the mercantile and she worried he'd come out and say, "What's all this?" and break the spell Bill

Doolin had cast over her.

He stood there, reins of his horse held lightly in a gloved hand, the other hand holding the sweat-stained Stetson down along one leg. Truth be told, he smelled a bit of sweat and horse and smoke, but that did not deter her from wanting to know more, to be in his company, to listen to wild tales of a cowboy's life.

They chatted for a few minutes more before her father appeared holding a wood box of foodstuffs, cans of peaches and beans with pork, a quarter of salted ham, flour, sugar, and such. The man looked first at Doolin then at his daughter then back at Doolin.

"Edith, would you care to introduce this gentleman?"

Her cheeks were still flushed as if they'd been stung by the cold.

"Father, this is Mr. Bill Doolin," she said demurely.

Bill settled his hat quickly back on his head and extended his hand to the man, noting as he did the preacher's clothes, the white collar befitting a black, if threadbare jacket.

Both men noted the strength in the other's grip.

"Doolin," her father said quizzically. "Seems I've heard that name before."

Without missing a beat Bill said, "Well, I wouldn't be surprised, sir. I'm known pretty much all over as a top hand."

"So you're a drover, then, what some call a cow puncher?"

At this Doolin nearly laughed, but held back and simply smiled broadly, the whiteness of his teeth showing through his heavy dark beard.

"I guess you could describe it as that—when I'm not mending fence or putting a new roof on something or mucking out horse stalls."

"Yes, well, we must be getting on," the preacher said. "It was a pleasure to meet you, Mr. Doolin."

Doolin could not keep his eyes off her.

As the preacher loaded the box of goods in the bed of a buckboard wagon, she whispered quickly, "We live in the white house beside the church."

He watched them go and she could feel Bill Doolin's eyes on her and it gave her great pleasure to think that he was so taken with her on first sight, just as she admitted in her room that night lying in the dark, she'd been taken with him. The thought of him quickened her heart until she told herself she was being a silly girl.

And now they were married and he was talking once more of moving, this time to New Mexico, so far, far away.

"What about father?" she asked.

Doolin shrugged.

"He's welcome to come along," he said.

"But he can't just leave his church."

"We'll work something out," he said.

He'd all along wanted to tell her the truth of his business, the fact that he pointed guns at folks and forced them to hand over their money, the fact that he was never ever going back to simply being a ranch hand or some store clerk. The fact that even if he'd wanted to, there was no way he could ever become an honest citizen. Heck Thomas most especially would never let him rest.

He tried envisioning life in a prison cell and the thought of it made him physically ill.

He wanted to reveal to his wife the sordid tale of his life and he wanted to tell her ever so badly that he'd as soon die as to be locked up knowing she was out there somewhere, subject to the efforts of other, freer men, to woo and win her heart. He could never ever tolerate the knowledge that she would be with any other man.

"I'd kill myself first, Edith," he wanted to say.

In New Mexico they could maybe get something of a fresh start. And if the law began to close in on him down there—Heck Thomas and them—why they could easily enough skip across the border. Then he would have to tell her the truth and he hoped that she loved him enough to accept it and not abandon him.

"We'll work out something," he said again with regard to her father.

"But right now, why don't we go get an ice cream cone and eat it on one of those park benches."

She smiled happily. Like a child. Like a beautiful child.

CHAPTER 18

Got a telephone call from a Marshal Seldon Lindsey over in Elk saying to scratch one more name off the Oklahombre list of terrifiers—Bill Dalton.

Said, "Me and Loss Hart, a deputy, surrounded a ranch owned by Huston Wallace near the Arbuckle Mountains near Elk here and caught Dalton out in the open.

"Upon our approach we saw a man playing with several children out front of the main house. We dismounted at a good distance so as not to be noticed by him thinking he could be Dalton, or one of his comrades who had recently robbed the bank in Longview, Texas, where a goodly number of people were shot, some killed in a bloody holdup.

"I told Loss to get down and we crawled to within a hundred yards of where Dalton, as it proved out and not some other, was hefting the children up on his shoulders and swinging them about by their arms.

"Don't shoot, Loss, I said, for you're liable to hit one of them youngsters. Loss was anxious because there was thirty thousand dollars reward money on Dalton and he could feel that money burning a hole in his pocket already.

"So we held our ground and couldn't see no way to get closer still without being discovered."

Seldon coughed once or twice, said he had caught a bad cold, then continued on.

"Well, one of them kids, a little girl it was, went running off right

toward where me and Loss was lying and sure enough she came right up on us, stood staring for a minute, seen our Winchesters and ran off screaming 'Daddy, daddy, there's some men with guns!'.

"Soon as he heard that he took off running, went straight into the house and me and Loss was running too trying to catch him. The kids were all screaming terrified and I cursed our poor luck for having to chase them babies' daddy, but there wasn't nothing could be done for it."

I listened with a sense of both relief and sorrow that those children would have to watch their daddy die. Don't care what a badman Dalton was, his kids were innocent in all this and I could only imagine what them youngsters must have thought.

Loss went on with the rest of it and I stood there one hand against the wall next to the telephone feeling like a man caught with one foot in the old ways and one in the new.

"Me and Loss pulled up short once he got inside the house, figuring he had guns in there and we sure as hell didn't want to get ambushed. I yelled for those kids to get the hell far gone as they could. Last thing I wanted was some dead child on my hands from a stray bullet.

"It didn't take long and we heard glass breaking around back, the busting of wood, and me and Loss went on around the side of the place in time to see Dalton rabbiting away. He'd crashed out a back window and still had glass in his hair. I called for him to halt, told him who I was. He had a revolver and turned and snapped off a shot at us and kept on going. Loss said, 'Shoot him now, boss?' I fired my Winchester and the round spun him about and Loss fired and knocked him over.

"We rolled over and sure enough it was Dalton. I knew him personally and there wasn't any doubt. Blood trickled from his mouth and he sort of smiled, believe it or not, like he was happy it was finally over and he would be leaving this old earth.

"I leaned down and said, 'Well, Bill, looks like you've robbed your last bank.'

"He coughed and spat a bloody wad and said, 'Yes, you're probably right, you pie-eyed bastard, but do you know how much we got from that Longview bank? Forty thousand dollars, which is more than you and the whole goddamn bunch of marshals are ever going to make.'

"I said, 'Well maybe so, Bill, but you'll have a tough time spending it in hell.' He coughed again and expired. His kids crying as they looked on. A woman then came from the house and took charge of them and called me and Loss everything but white men. I never heard a woman cuss so bad."

Seldon paused and I could hear his ragged breathing on the other end of the line and once more thought what a miracle it was two folks could talk to one another so many miles apart.

"Just thought you'd like to know, Heck," he said. "One less miscreant you have to waste a bullet on."

We said our so longs and rang off. I could not wait to go and tell the big Dane and Tilghman the good news, wanted to tell them in person and not over some goddamn device nobody knew how it worked. The last of the Daltons had purchased himself a ticket on the Devil's express and now most of the brothers, but for Emmitt still in prison, were laid to rest. The ranks of the Wild Bunch were thinning and I did not believe it would be very much longer before they were all rubbed out or serving time in a jailhouse. At least I hoped it wouldn't.

I would later learn that Dalton had broken off from Doolin's bunch and formed his own gang. I'd heard it said of Dalton that he was bitter and never got over the fact that Doolin had refused to ride with his brothers that day into Coffeyville. And though he'd yoked himself to Doolin, he did not intend to keep it that way. Trouble was, like his dead brothers, seemed like Bill Dalton wasn't much good at planning his crimes.

My wife came in then and asked who it was called. I told her and she wiped her hands on her apron and shook her head and said she wished I'd find another line of work, that she feared someday somebody would bring me home in the back of a wagon under a tarpaulin, my muddy boots sticking out.

"I don't know what I'd do if I lost you, Heck."

I tried reassuring her that I'd come up against some pretty bad actors in my time and I wasn't dead yet and she ought not to worry and asked if she'd fix me a cup of coffee while I went out to saddle my mare, that I was going to ride over and see the big Dane and Bill Tilghman and tell them the news.

"Why don't you just call them?" she said.

I just smiled and patted her on the bottom.

I felt like smoking a cigar.

Chapter 19

Doolin was mending a harness when Bitter Creek came riding up on a large claybank gelding and dismounted. He had the look of a man carrying with him bad news.

"Dalton's been killed by lawmen," he said. "Over in Elk, two days back. Shot him down like a dog. Never even gave him a chance to surrender."

Doolin listened passively, said, "Shit, Dalton was too ignorant to surrender. Knowing him, he wanted to take as many of them laws as he could for what happened to his brothers."

"They robbed this bank over in Longview, shot up the citizenry. I guess they didn't like it much and ultimately tracked him down."

"Well, so be it," Bill said. "You want something to eat?"

"Sure."

Bill called to the house and when Edith appeared he asked if she'd fix Bitter Creek a plate of victuals. Wordlessly she disappeared inside again. She never liked most of Bill's friends. They seemed rough and uncouth and dangerous to her. She wondered why Bill would have gone into the cattle business with such men, but then told herself it was because only such rough-looking characters would know how to find and trade cattle—that no gentleman such as Bill could sometimes be.

"How's Rose?" Bill said idly, still repairing the harness.

"Me and her are on the outs again," Bitter Creek said glumly, taking out his pipe and tobacco pouch and filling the bowl.

"What's that they say," Bill said, "how true love never runs smooth?"

"Wasn't that I crave her so much I'd be in the wind," George said, holding the flame of a match to the bowl and sucking on the stem of the pipe till it caught.

"She is a thing of nubile beauty," Bill said, remembering how he'd last seen her, the outline of her body within the thin shift she'd worn that day, those small breasts like pears.

"I bet she gives you the fits, don't she, George?"

"She's like some sort of bad habit I can't quit."

Edith came out with a plate of salted pork, biscuit, and beans and handed it to Bitter Creek, who said, "Thankee, Edith."

"You're welcome," she said and turned and went back to the house.

"I'm hungry enough to eat the ears off a donkey," Bitter Creek said.

"Well, lucky for me I've got no donkeys to eat the ears off of."

"Lucky for the donkeys," Bitter Creek joked.

Bill watched him eat and smoke at the same time, like a man who couldn't stop doing either.

"When you reckon you'll be ready to get back to it?" George said, wiping his mouth with the cuff of his shirt.

"I reckon any time now. We'll ride on into town and send word to the others to come on."

"They's something else," Bitter Creek said, scraping the last of his beans up into his maw. "Them goddamn brothers of Rose's."

"What about them?"

"I don't trust 'em."

"What makes you say that?" Bill said, punching a thick needle through the harness's leather to complete the repair.

"They've been out on the scout for fellas with reward money, more'n usual."

"And you're thinking they might come after us?"

"I'm thinking those sons a bitches would come after their own ma if there was a reward on her."

"Then you best be careful around them," Bill said.

"I mean they never treat me with anything but respect, even if grudgingly so," Bitter Creek said, setting aside his scraped plate and relighting his pipe. "But that's because Rose is their sister and she's protective of me and I don't think they'd try anything and suffer her wrath. Hell I sometimes think Dal and some of them is in love with her, the way they are all the time watching her whenever they come around."

"How do they watch her?" Bill said, more out of curiosity than anything.

"Like a man watches a woman he wants to get up in," Bitter Creek said. "Not like a brother would usually watch his sister. Jesus."

"Those Dunns never did look right to me," Bill said. "They always seemed a little off in the head."

"Well, they best not come up on me or I'll shoot their goddamn eyes out."

"Might be better was you to shoot their dicks off," Bill laughed.

"Might," George laughed along with him. "Shit. I'm feeling in need of some action. Let's go steal something."

"Let's," Bill said, looking back toward the house. "I'll tell Edith that you came because there was a big cattle sale going on down in Kansas."

"You think she knows you're lying to her?"

Bill shrugged.

"She might, but on the other hand, I treat her and her daddy right, take care of 'em, and maybe it's best if you know a thing that might not be quite right that you don't say nothing just to get along."

Bitter Creek contemplated that and said, "Jesus, Bill, you sometimes befuddle my brains."

"It's that young pussy that's got you soft-brained," Bill said with a devious smile.

"I can't argue with you there," George said, knocking the ash from his pipe on the bottom of his boot heel. "She's half my age and I ain't but twenty eight years old, though it seems sometimes like I'm a hundred."

Bill went into the house and in a little while came out again carrying his saddlebags over one shoulder, a Winchester in his hand. He went to the corral and roped out the bloodbay gelding and saddled it. Slid the Winchester down into the saddle sock and stepped into the saddle. George was waiting for him, leaned forward, forearms resting on his saddle horn staring toward the house, toward Edith who stood in the doorway watching them cautiously.

Bill rode over and spoke something to her out of George's earshot then turned and rode back and said, "Let's go."

George was thinking all this talk had gotten him thirsty and horned up. There was this gal in Stillwater, if she still worked there, he figured to pay a visit to while they awaited the arrival of the rest of the boys, Tulsa Blake and the others.

He said to Bill as they rode out, "Rose ain't the only hen in the henhouse, you know."

"Don't tell me you aim to visit Fatima?"

"I damn well aim it."

Bill shook his head.

"You are one faithless son of a bitch," Bill said.

"I am, ain't I?" George said. "I mean why waste all this on just one woman, anyway?"

"Guns and money," Bill said. "It's what we do."

"Don't forget the pussy," George said.

"Not my concern," Bill said. "I'm a happily married man."

"Most of the time."

"Most of the time," Bill said.

Thunder clouds were building in the west over the Arbuckles, a pretty sight for those lucky enough to see it.

CHAPTER 20

Dal Dunn paid his sister a visit.

"What's wrong with you, gal?"

The right side of her face was bruised the color of a half-ripe plum.

"Oh George and me had a falling-out," she said. "Sometimes he can be so mean."

"That right?"

"He . . ."

"He what?"

"He slapped me. He was drinking and he wasn't in his right mind, Dal. Please don't say nothing to the others."

"I'm going to kill that son of a bitch for hitting you."

"No," she pleaded, grabbing hold of his shirt sleeve as if to hold him back. He looked at her and old fever arose in him, a fever he didn't ever want to admit he had. She was the comeliest gal he ever had been around and she did something to him he knew was unnatural as hell.

"Leave go of me," Dal said. "I'm going to track that bastard down and make him pay."

She refused to unhand him lest he shove her off.

"Hell," he said. "What you see in a man like him, anyway? He's almost twice your age and ugly as a mule."

"I love him, Dal. I love him."

"Well, he obviously don't feel the same about you or he wouldn't go smacking you around, little as you are and good as you treat him."

"It ain't all his fault," she continued to plead. "I get his goat 'cause I know I can. If I just didn't say nothing to rile him everything would be okay."

"It ain't okay for a man to strike a woman," Dal said with all indignity.

"No, no. It's okay sometimes 'cause sometimes I deserve it, I do, Dal. I deserve it. Otherwise George treats me good, but sometimes I deserve it."

"Ah, hell," Dal said, feeling defeated by her pleading. "There's plenty of other men who'd love on you good, Rose. You know that. Pretty little thing as you are."

Their eyes locked for a moment too long, then she let go of his sleeve and his arm fell at his side, the anger in him abated somewhat, standing there staring at her.

"What is it you want, Dal?"

The way she said it, the look in her eyes, left him tongue tied.

"Nothing," he said.

"You crave me, don't you, Dal?"

"Don't talk crazy like that," he protested.

"A woman can tell," she said.

"You can't tell nothing about what I'm thinking or not thinking."

"Yes, I can," she said. "I've seen that look in your eyes for some time now."

She was acting coy now but he couldn't rightly tell if it was just to calm him down, get his mind on other things than killing Newcomb or what.

"You ain't seen no look in my eyes," he said. "Never."

"Okay," she said. "I didn't. But I know I did."

"Listen," he said harshly, looking toward the door as if fearful one of the others would come in and hear them and see them like this. "You leave off with such talk lest Bee and them think

I'm some sort of goddamn . . ." He couldn't find the word for it.

"I won't tell nothing," she said. "Long as you leave George be."

"What's that supposed to mean?"

"Just this," she said and raised her shift to show full on her nakedness. "I don't mind you want to do it with me now and again when George ain't around, but you got to promise to leave him be."

He felt rivulets of sweat trickle down his ribs underneath his shirt. He made pretense of trying to look away.

"Put your dress down, Rose, what in the hell is wrong with you?"

"Tell me you don't care for what you see, Dal."

"Oh, goddamn leave me be."

He stormed outside and walked all over the compound unsure of exactly what he was doing other than trying to un-think what he'd been thinking. He looked twice back at Rose and George's cabin then went into the dimness of the barn with its fecundity of hay and horse. He hove away in the darkest part of the barn and fumbled with himself, tugging and pulling away until he was relieved of his pent-up anguish, then sagged down onto a bed of straw and lay there staring up into the rafters, their beams of light pouring down from missing shingles, the dancing dust moats in the beams like some sort of pixie dust.

He liked it there in the barn and now spent, he closed his eyes and fell asleep and thought no more of killing Bitter Creek Newcomb that day.

Rose had gotten a perverse thrill out of showing her brother Dal her nakedness. She enjoyed the thought of any man looking at her, lusting after her, kin or no, though she much preferred the idea that it was a man not blood related.

Bitter Creek was all the time telling her how desirous he was of her, how much he enjoyed the smallness of her frame, calling her sometimes his "child baby." But she often wondered what other men might think or say about her to see her fully naked, had wondered since she'd turned a teenager and sexually aware of her allures.

She sat and laughed over having run Dal off with the simple exposure of her, knew she held power over him now. Wondered if such of a woman's power wasn't all in her body alone. Maybe that's the way God gave us women an equal chance, she thought. That and a good Colt revolver.

She wondered when George might return, longed for him, cursed him in between the longing. Couldn't abide with him, couldn't abide without him. Same thing he'd often said to her.

"Well, damn it!" she said.

"Who you talking to?"

She turned around and there was her eldest brother, Bill.

It surprised her. She hadn't even heard him come in.

"Nobody," she said. "Myself."

"You seen Dal?" Bill said. "I need him to come on with us."

She shook her head.

"Thought I seen him heading over here earlier."

She shrugged.

"Ain't seen him," she said.

"What happened to your face? Newcomb do that to you?"

"No, I bumped it on the edge of a door in the middle of the night."

Bill eyed her suspiciously.

"Well, maybe you did something to deserve it," he said. "Women can be a caution to any man and I doubt Newcomb is any exception."

She flushed angry but held her tongue. Bill was wily and knew how to bait someone into something before they knew it.

"Yes, I could have," she said, "but I didn't. I run into the damn door standing open."

He nodded.

"You see Dal before I do, tell him to come on," he said and turned and left out. Never even gave her a second look.

To hell with you all, she thought. *Ever goddamn one of you men.*

CHAPTER 21

Doolin became a ghost, him and his bunch hitting places here and there and everywhere and then slinking off and laying low for a time as though they never existed at all.

They hit a train in Dover, Oklahoma, in April while the rest of us were in church, our kids finding Easter eggs in the grass while their folks cheered them on, and generally living like the good decent folks that we all were. I reckon outlaws don't take much time off to celebrate such as the Lord's crucifixion or nothing else for that matter.

We went after them once more, Chris and me with about twenty men, but Doolin and the others were long into the wind. Witnesses described them well enough that we knew it was Doolin and Bitter Creek Newcomb leading them and probably Red Buck Weightman and Tulsa Blake along and some others we'd not yet had a handle on. We showed a passel of dodgers and some of the extra names came like "Little" Dick West and Bill Raidler. The names and faces of that Wild Bunch kept changing but the intent stayed the same.

There could have been more in among them that robbed the train but such confusion reigned as it usually does in an armed robbery that it was hard to tell precisely who all was with Doolin.

The big Dane grumbled and swore an oath that he was damn sick and tired of being outslicked by a bunch of damn miscreants, said it would take a lawman or two guarding every bank and train in the country if we were to catch them.

"Damn it to hell, Heck. I'm about ready to pull out my hair!"

I said he ought not do that since he didn't have none too much to spare in trying to keep him steady. Said, "Enough reward money's put up, they'll turn each other in to collect it. There's no such thing as honor among thieves when a man knows he can get rich by just writing a name on a piece of paper. Some of those boys would write their own mas' names down if they thought they could get paid for it."

"I ain't so sure as you are, Heck," he replied while we ate our supper in a Dover hotel that was nothing but a damn firetrap as dry and unpainted as it was. The food was bad, the liquor worse, and I don't even want to say about how homely the whores were in that town. We could not wait to leave there once we sent word out through the telegraph wires for everyone within three hundred miles to be on the lookout for Bill Doolin and any man riding with him. We had their photographs printed up on dodgers, which was one of those modern-day aids we had over the old days where all you had to go by was some rendering of what a fellow looked like that usually could look like just about anybody. The Pinkertons had perfected the technique of adding photographs to the dodgers. I figured there would come a day when a man couldn't swipe an apple without the law being able to catch him the way things were developing, what with photographs and telephones and the like.

We joined up with the local sheriff and chased hoof prints we believed belong to the hombres until the trail went cold and once more we were forced to give up the chase.

The Dane said he didn't know how much more he could take of chasing ghosts. I said, "Well, we got Ol Yantis and Bill Dalton and not too long back they got Ned Christie too. That bunch right there puts something of a dent in these outlaws, don't they?"

He nodded as we'd sauntered on down the street from the hotel upon our return of six days out on the trail, and were sipping whiskey there in the local saloon to ease our troubled minds.

Neither Chris nor myself was much partakers in the demon rum, but on occasion, just to buoy our spirits, we'd have us a taste, long as the stuff was good. The barkeep said the best he had was something called Old Number 7, a whiskey made in Lynchburg, Tennessee. Shit, it wasn't too bad, neither. Smooth as a hooker's silk underdrawers, Chris said. I said, what would you know about a hooker's underdrawers? He grinned and said, Shucks, Heck, there's a hell of a lot I know about a hell of a lot you might not guess I know about.

I said I doubted that and we ordered one more glass for the road then each headed on to our respective homes and waiting wives and warm, soft beds.

Every day, week, month, and year that passed it was getting harder to sleep out on the hard ground and eat campfire grub, and wasn't none of us getting any younger far as we could tell. Chasing outlaws was becoming more and more like a young man's game and we sure enough wished we'd hurry up and rub out the current bunch of blackguards before we retired.

But truth was, we didn't seem to be making enough progress to protect the good folks in I.T. or Oklahoma. Every time you picked up the newspaper there was another story about misdeeds:

TULSA MAN MURDERS WIFE AND CHILDREN WITH AX
CHICKSAW COUPLE ROBBED & MURDERED
EUFAULA WOMAN RAPED BY GANG
ARDMORE BANK ROBBED, TWO KILLED IN SHOOTOUT
INNOCENT BYSTANDER GUNNED DOWN IN LENAPAH

Hells bells, I said to Edith. It's getting so I don't even like reading the paper anymore.

Then don't read it, she said.

I won't.

Then good.

How else am I to know what's going on around here if I don't read the paper?

I guess you either read it or you don't, but it seems to give you a bad case of dyspepsia every time you do and we've about run through a hundred dollars' worth of bicarbonate this month alone.

She was kidding, of course. But probably not by much.

I don't know why I just didn't quit it all, but I just didn't, couldn't, wouldn't.

There is something about pinning on a badge and swearing an oath to uphold the law. Something about keeping your word and doing the work most others wouldn't.

Something about staying honest that seemed to me a lot less work than running crooked and all the time having to look over your shoulder. Like cheating on your wife, the way some men will do and living with a guilty conscience and that never did appeal to my sensibilities.

Chris and Bill Tilghman were cut from the same cloth as me. We might not have been perfect but we were sure a long way from being outlaws.

We also knew our odds of getting shot to pieces someday were pretty good too but it didn't scare us any. Most of us had been shot or cut with a knife already.

You might wonder why men like us would take on such work since the pay was paltry, but for the reward money we might share. I can't answer you on that but to say it gave us a sense we were doing God's work, I guess you could say—being thy brother's keeper as it were.

It was rewarding knowing we eliminated bad men from the society of decent folks.

Oh, don't get me wrong, there was other rewards for us too such as being spoken about in a good light by your peers and coming home to a loving wife and having her throw her arms around your neck and tell you how happy she was to see you safe and sound. Sitting down to a home-cooked meal after weeks out on the trail. Then later going on to the bedroom and making up for all that missed time.

Yes, sir. I don't regret it.

Chapter 22

Another bank, but this time not so good.

The modus operandi was the same: Tulsa Blake holding the horses while the others went in guns drawn, hammers cocked back, pointed and aimed accompanied by dire threats: "Your money or your life!"

Blake sitting a stolen paint horse, then a sudden eruption of gunfire from within. An accountant figuring it time to become a gunfighter turned the bank into a meat grinder.

The accountant was instantly shot dead by Red Buck Weightman who enjoyed the killing almost as much as he did the robbing. Screamed at the corpse amid the melee, "Take that, you dumb son of a bitch!"

Unfortunately for Doolin, however, the accountant's aim wild as it was still glanced off Doolin's skull, spinning him sideways before slamming him to the plank floor. Jesus but that floor sure came up fast. The accountant, cum gunfighter, had been a family man and a member of the local Masonic Lodge until the very moment he decided to become brave.

The gunfire had the same effect as ringing the town's fire bell, drew forth from inside shops and saloon fronts armed citizenry, some of them yelling: "They're robbing the bank!" A familiar refrain in those times and towns, and the locals came running with everything from pocket pistols to shotguns, all firing wildly, shooting at any living thing before them.

A workhorse hitched to a buckboard was blown over by a

man firing both hammers of a twelve-dollar Sears Roebuck shotgun. He'd loaded the shells with dimes 'cause he heard that's what Billy the Kid had slain two lawmen with—a shotgun loaded with dimes.

A woman was nicked in the ankle by a splinter of wood from the lintel of a millinery she was seeking to duck into. A kid who'd been rolling a hoop had his shoe heel shot off and went hopping and yelling like a scalded dog.

Tulsa Blake was trying to hold the gang's skittish horses with one hand and fire his gun with the other. He was having trouble with both, yelled, "Come on!" to the boys as they hustled outside, Little Bill Raidler under one of Doolin's arms and Dynamite Dick Clifton under the other. Red Buck Weightman backed out of the bank still firing into it. Tulsa Blake figured Doolin killed when he saw the free flow of blood streaming down his face. Just then Red Buck turned and shot a man in a gray vest, felling him face first into a horse trough. A bullet clipped Tulsa Blake's Stetson and spun it sideways.

Doolin's head rang like there were church bells gonging in it and he was so dizzy he was sick to his stomach and had a hard time holding onto his horse once lifted aboard. Tulsa Blake rode alongside helping to prop him up, shouting, "Hang in there, Bill. We'll make it."

The entire action took under fifteen minutes from start to finish. In the gang's wake, there were dead and wounded, their groans and cries as if after the passing of a terrible storm.

The gang rode until their horses near gave out. They abandoned the main roads and cut through woods and down into coulees and out again and across streams and over rocks. Anything they could to shake off any pursuing posse.

They rode into darkness and slept in their saddles, letting the horses have their head and set a walking pace. They rested only long enough to give their mounts a blow and water.

They kept going for days all the time watching their back trail.

Finally, they took refuge in a sand basin along the Cimarron because Doolin was unable to ride further and the rest were pretty worn down and needed the rest, man and horse non-negotiable.

They figured they'd shaken the town's dust from their feet and were in the clear by then. Posses weren't by nature all that eager to be gone on the scout for a very long time, at least those not sworn and paid by the law.

They patched up Doolin's head wound as best as they could and Little Bill had a busted thumb that caused him to wince and cuss every time he banged it against anything, said it hurt to even hold his pecker to take a piss.

"Well they sure as hell put up a fight," Red Buck said begrudgingly.

"Them hayseeds wasn't about to give it up easy, was they?" Dynamite Dick said, resting on his bootheels by the edge of the camp's smokeless fire. He idly stirred the gray ashes with a green stick.

"No, they sure as hell wasn't," Red Buck said.

Tulsa Blake nursed Doolin like a mother a child, dipped a cloth in the river, wrung it out some, and returned and placed it on Doolin's bruised and swollen forehead.

"Another inch and we'd had to scoop your brains up with a teaspoon," he joked, but the joke didn't set well with Doolin.

"Feels like somebody took a ballpeen hammer to my skull."

Red Buck looked at him rather mercilessly, said, "We ought to keep on moving."

Doolin was half feverish and had hardly any fight in him. More and more lately Red Buck was proving to be rancorous and hard to take his onerous ways.

"We'll stay as long as it takes to get Bill feeling better and rest our mounts," Blake said in that overprotective way. "We push any harder right now, we'll be walking the rest of the way home."

"You maybe," Red Buck said.

"Ain't nobody holding a gun to you if you want to go."

"No, there sure as hell ain't and the last one who tried it ended up leaving his wife a widow, now didn't he?"

The others looked off or stared into the fire and didn't say anything, didn't choose one side or the other, but every one of them knew that as it almost always did, a gang's leader would always be challenged at some point, especially if he was in a weakened state.

Doolin shifted his gaze and leveled it on Red Buck. Then said to Tulsa Blake, "Give him his cut."

"We ain't begun yet to divide up the money," Blake said.

"Give him his cut and let him go on."

"You sure, Bill?"

The others listened without letting on that they were.

"Give it to him."

"Fine by me," Red Buck said. "I don't want to be sitting here holding my dick in my hands when that posse catches up with us 'cause one of us ain't fit to ride."

Blake got the money from the bank bag and counted it into even stacks then handed Red Buck his.

"Anybody else want to turn tail?" he said.

Blake might be Bill's toady, but he was just as dangerous as any of the rest of them.

Nobody said anything.

Red Buck stuffed his share into his shirt, stood, and without a further word went and saddled his horse and rode off.

"Good riddance," Blake said to nobody in particular. "We'll take turns standing watch, the rest of us get some rest."

Night sounds drifted up from the river, the croak of frogs,

the flat splash of a mud turtle or fish, the slobber of water in the shallow places.

Doolin dreamed fevered dreams. In one he had died and was lying in a rough-hewn coffin of plain pine planks. Edith stood over him, her cheeks sallow and streaked with tears. She kept saying, "Why, Bill, why?"

Her father was there too, his face creased with disappointment at the man he'd allowed his only daughter to marry. Somebody was singing in the background, old hymns that were heart tugging and it gave him the greatest sadness to hear them.

He came awake and looked about and nobody was moving, the others rolled up in their blankets but for the night watch of whom he could not see there in the darkness.

He tried to sit up but his head felt like the weight of an anvil. He lay there silent, breathing, sweating, struck through with sharp searing pain. He found himself breathing faster than he ought to, the breathing of a fearful man, and yet he was not fearful.

What's wrong with me? he asked himself. *Goddamn it, what's wrong with me?*

He fell asleep again and woke to the sound of someone shouting. It was Tulsa Blake warning, "They're coming! There's a posse coming! You boys make a run for it. Somebody help Bill get on his horse."

Then the crack of a rifle, Blake's Winchester as he fired at something unseen by the others as Dynamite Dick and Bill Raidler lifted Doolin to his feet and onto his horse. They had left the horses saddled overnight for just such an emergency.

"Run!" Blake said between rifle shots. Bullets splatted the sand and spewed small water jets when they struck the river.

"I'll hold these sons a bitches long as I can hold 'em!" Blake declared with bravado. He was the one on watch. It was his duty to cover for the escape of the rest.

Bill and them splashed across the ankle-deep river to the other side and lost themselves in among canebrakes, the gunfire growing dimmer and dimmer as they made their escape. Bill's head throbbed worse than ever and he was mad to simply hold onto the saddle's horn and keep his seat as they fled.

It wasn't long before they were out of earshot of the gunfire.

That, or the fight back at the sand pit was over.

Nobody was willing to wait around and see which. Bill kept telling himself, "Ol Blake can take care of himself. I don't need to worry about Ol Blake."

CHAPTER 23

I was visited today by a deputy marshal name of Will Banks who said he'd been in the fight down on the Cimarron where he and a posse had tracked Doolin's bunch after they robbed the bank in Southwest City, Missouri. Said he had a daughter nearby over in Ardmore and thought he'd tell me personal that he'd killed Tulsa Blake in the shootout and that he and his group had wounded two or three of the other gang's members but he couldn't be sure which or who they were by name.

"That son of a buck put up a hell of a fight," he said, "I'll give him that."

"Well, that is good news," I said, "here's to you and your boys."

He didn't act proud.

"Never liked to kill anybody if I could bring them in alive, Heck," he said.

"I know it," I said. "We're just lawmen trying to do the best we can with cleaning up this country. You sure Doolin was with them?"

"Can't be sure a hundred percent, but we found bloody rags in their camp. Far as I know Doolin was the only one who took a wound at that bank job."

Banks was a smallish, unassuming man with sandy hair and moustaches who, if dressed in better clothes, might be mistaken for a banker himself.

"They killed some people in that robbery," he said, "otherwise we might not have tracked them so hard."

"They don't fool around, do they?" I said.

"No, they sure don't."

"Would you stay for supper?" I said. "It's the least I could owe you for making a side trip over and telling me the news personal."

"I'd sure enough like to," he said, "but I best be getting on. My girl is pregnant with her first child and my wife is waiting for me over at the hotel so we can get on over there."

"Yes, sir," I said. "Family is important."

He nodded and we shook hands and I walked him out.

"We'll get them all sooner or later, Heck," he said with a great degree of confidence but without braggadocio.

"Damned if we won't," I said.

I went in and telephoned Chris Madsen to tell him the news but his wife said he was out on the scout for some wanted men. So I called over and told Bill Tilghman.

"I already heard about it," he said. "Read about it in the newspaper. We've bagged another one."

"We got some real good men out on the scout," I said.

"We do, sure enough."

"Knocking 'em down like ten pins," I said.

He grunted, said, "I hope we don't run out too soon, I could use the reward money for a new place I'm building over near Guthrie, closer to my wife's people," he said.

"You sure you want to do that, be close to a mother-in-law?" I joked.

"Hell, I reckon there is worse things," he laughed. "She bakes good rhubarb pies."

"Well, that's something."

"Keep your powder dry, Heck, till we run into each other again—hopefully at ol' Bill Doolin's funeral."

"Might be a possibility," I said and rang off.

I went out into the evening air, the sky the prettiest softest shade of red I'd ever seen, and smoked a cigar. Things were looking better all the time. Every one of the miscreants we arrested or put in the ground made for one less we'd have to deal with later on.

I reckoned Doolin's gang was getting skinny with every loss of manpower and hoped that maybe he'd see the handwriting on the wall and give himself up.

So what happened next caught me by surprise.

Chapter 24

Doolin, home again with Edith who nursed his head wound, wondered if maybe it was time to get out of the game. He'd learned of the death of Tulsa Jack and felt disheartened that Jack, next to Bitter Creek Newcomb, was his closest friend and ally.

"They're going to kill us all," he muttered to himself there on the sun-filled front porch of the house they rented and shared with her father.

"What's that you say, Bill?" Edith asked. She'd been sitting next to him knitting and only paying the slightest attention.

He realized he'd spoken in her presence his fear of being murdered by lawmen.

"Nothing, sweet."

"No, I distinctly heard you say something about somebody killing you all."

His gaze flicked away toward some hills whose slopes were blackened by a recent grass fire. When the wind would shift it would carry with it the charred smell.

"There's something I need to tell you," he said.

"Like how you got that head wound?" she said.

"Yes, it has to do with that."

"You and those others have been engaged in illegal activity, isn't that it, Bill?"

He looked over at her, at those intense gray-blue eyes that could turn fire and ice depending on her mood.

He nodded.

"Oh, Bill," she sighed heavily. "I knew it. I just knew that you had been all this while . . ."

"I should have told you from the outset," he said softly. "I just didn't want you to have to fret and worry over me."

"I *have* fretted over you. I've never stopped fretting over you every time you leave out and I don't see or hear from you for weeks at a time."

"Well, I'm sorry. I truly am."

They sat then in silence for a while, each with their own thoughts, Bill half relieved and half worried that now that she knew, whether or not his wife would stick by him.

She looked solemn, broken, weighted under the yoke of truth now that he'd confirmed her worse fears.

"I knew you couldn't make as much money as you did simply being in the cattle business," she said at last. "I'm no fool, Bill Doolin, in spite of what you might think."

"No, I never thought of you as any fool," he said, "except for marrying me."

"I don't regret that. I love you."

"I wouldn't blame you if you chose to leave me now that you know the truth."

For a moment longer she didn't say anything. Then: "How bad is it, Bill?"

"Bad," he said. "They killed Tulsa Blake two weeks ago."

"Jack?"

He nodded as if ashamed for the killing. Blake had covered their escape and paid for it with his life. You couldn't ask for a better friend than that.

Her eyes misted over. She'd always liked Jack Blake.

"What are we to do?" she said.

"I'm reckoning as soon as I'm able and can put together a stake we head off to New Mexico."

"Father isn't well to travel," she said.

"We'll think of something."

She'd lost all heart for knitting, for the normal things in life. She wanted to ask her husband if he'd killed anyone himself, but she thought surely she already knew the answer to that and did not want to hear him admit to it—not that.

The sun burned hot in the sky, hotter than he reckoned he'd ever felt it. The light of it crossed the porch and touched his boots then slow as a snake climbed up his legs and into his lap and touched his hands and he reflexively withdrew them. Edith rose and went inside the house, her face drawn, her mouth grim. She let the screened door slap shut and it sounded like a pistol shot and caused him to flinch.

He wished Bitter Creek would come on from wherever he was. He could use a good friend right now, someone who understood what it was like to live in his skin.

The damn headaches.

In no time at all, without the appearance of Bitter Creek Newcomb, Doolin had his wife packed, leaving her father in care of a neighbor, and rode the buckboard off to the southwest with the intent of laying low in New Mexico.

It was a solemn ride with little conversation exchanged between husband and wife. Evenings would find them camped near some creek or river tributary gathered around a lone campfire that flickered in the darkness like Diogenes' lonely lamp.

They would eat, Bill gathering firewood and Edith fixing supper, their features batting in and out of the fire's dancing flames, hardly speaking at all except for Bill complimenting her on her ability to fix such good meals under such hard circumstances, to which she might say thank you, but not much else.

"Though the times are bad for us," he would say in the night, the two of them huddled under blankets in that high cold air, "we are still husband and wife and owe each other our vows of commitment" and he would take her and she would in silence yield to his taking her. But it was almost a dull passionless lovemaking that they shared. She could not get beyond the fact that he might have killed men for money, that his hands upon her breasts were a murderer's hands, that his mouth upon her mouth had spoken lies to her.

It was impossible for her to respond to him with the passion she once had when she believed him to be this other man.

Doolin had too much respect for her to force her to pretend that she wanted him more than she did, that she wanted him at all. He knew better. The tearing of trust was his doing and only his doing and he would take responsibility for that.

It was enough, what little she allowed, and later they would lie side by side staring up into the distant heavens, the blackest nights salted with a million stars, the smear of galaxies, and occasionally a shooting star, but not one they could wish upon.

He would stay awake until he heard the soft purring of her sleep, and then and only then would close his own eyes and fall into a fitful rest.

Each night was the same and each morning. Fall asleep after intercourse, rise at first light, fix a small fire, heat coffee, fry strips of bacon, biscuits in a Dutch oven, wash in the creek, harness the horse, and drive on.

The journey seemed endless and only occasionally did they come to a town or settlement where they might rent a room for a night and eat a meal in a café.

Bill was sorely tempted to drink, to get roaring drunk, but he did not for Edith's sake. He was already in the doghouse with her and didn't know when he would get out again.

They would stay and move on.

Finally, they reached Las Vegas in New Mexico and Bill said,

"We're here."

They found a small house to rent just off the plaza and things felt better at last.

Soon they were talking again and sharing their days, with Bill taking her to the bailes there in the plaza, the music and dancing lifting her spirits until at last she said to him, "I forgive you, Bill, but don't ever lie to me again. Ever."

He nodded, said that he would not, said that she knew everything there was to know about him.

She eyed him and said, "I doubt that, but I know now all the important stuff. I want to send for Father."

He said he would arrange it.

He did not know, could not know, that Bitter Creek and Charlie Pierce had paid the ultimate price for their sins while he danced with Edith in the town plaza in and out of the luminaries' flickering lights.

CHAPTER 25

"Boys, we got us a prize hog just waiting to be slaughtered," Bill Dunn said to his brothers, Bee, Calvin, Dal, and George.

"How so?" Bee said.

"Bitter Creek and them," he said.

"You aiming to collect the reward on Newcomb?"

"I damn well am and anyone who might be with him."

"How much is it?" Dal said.

"Five thousand goddamn dollars is what it is."

George Dunn whistled between spaced front teeth. "Shit," he said. "That's a boodle of money."

"Damn right it is," Bill said.

"When you planning on collecting it?"

"Soon as he comes back to visit Rose."

Dal's fevered hopes rose. Killing Rose's paramour would leave her without a man to care for her. He figured who better to care for her than himself, something he had always wanted.

"Let me be the first to put a bullet in him," Dal said.

"Is that how you're aiming to do it?" Bee said to Bill. "Kill him instead of arresting him?"

"What do you think?" Bill said. "You think Newcomb's the kind to just quit the game 'cause I asked him to?"

"Nah, I reckon we got to kill him," Dal said.

"Then it's settled," Bill said. "It's a thousand a piece when we turn his body in for the reward."

"Shit, this calls for a drink," Bee said.

They sauntered over to the local saloon and ordered drinks all around.

"And none of that rotgut, either," Bee said. "Make it the good stuff."

Newcomb reined in just shy of the Dunn compound. It was an hour till dusk and he wondered if maybe it was best to go in after dark in case there were any laws snooping around the place.

"What we waiting for?" Charlie Pierce said. "There's the goddamn house. I'm hungry enough to eat my own goddamn hat."

Still Newcomb sat, watchful, two revolvers stuck in his belt and a Winchester slid down in his saddle sock. Charlie Pierce was similarly armed.

"You think Rose might be able to get me a friend for the night?" Charlie asked. "It ain't only food I'm hungering for."

Newcomb said, "Shit, everything looks okay to me. I don't see no laws running around," and spurred his mount forward with Charlie alongside him.

"Goddamn I'm about wore to the bone," Charlie complained as they neared the house where Rose stayed. "I don't know even if I had a gal for tonight I could even fuck her, tired as I am."

Newcomb remained watchful. Something didn't seem quite right, but on the other hand there was nothing he saw that led him to believe anything was wrong.

The sun rested on the horizon like an orange spilled from a basket.

They reined in at the house and Doolin and Charlie dismounted. Usually Rose was right there to greet him, to throw herself into his arms. It just didn't feel right.

"Something's wrong, Charlie," Newcomb said as Charlie stood beside his horse.

"What?"

"I don't know."

Then Dal Dunn stepped from within the house.

"Howdy, George."

George jerked one of his revolvers but Bill Dunn stepped from around one of the nearby structures and shot him through the guts with his Winchester.

Newcomb folded up and sat down hard, his hands trying to hold in the blood even as the rest of him went numb.

Charlie scrambled for his own gun and both Bee and George shot him at the same time with their Winchesters, one round taking off part of his face—cheek to jowl bone, and the other bursting his heart. He was dead before he hit the ground. And yet another round slammed into Newcomb, fired from Dal's pistol into him.

Then there was just silence as the sun melted into the earth and darkness came on like a stalking panther.

"It's done," Bill Dunn said. "Yonder lies a shitload of money. Let's get 'em loaded into the wagon and haul their asses in to the sheriff.

Which is what they did.

Halfway to the sheriff's, Newcomb opened his eyes. His body was afire, the pain more than any man should have to bear. He cried out. Dal, who was riding on the buckboard's seat with brother Bill, turned and stared down at him.

"Shit if Newcomb ain't still alive," he said. "What you want me to do, Bill?"

"Shoot him again."

Dal removed his revolver from the holster on his hip, aimed and cocked it as he pointed it straight at Newcomb's head. Newcomb looked up into the black maw of the gun.

"You son of a bitch . . ."

It was as much a sigh as it was a declaration and Dal happily squeezed the trigger, the bullet cracking open Newcomb's forehead like an egg. The shot spooked the wagon horses and it was all Bill Dunn could do to rein them in.

"Is he dead this time?" he growled.

"Looks to be, some of his brains is spilled out," Dal said.

"Good."

Town Marshal Canton was perched on a chair out front of the jail studying the streets as if expecting some sort of miracle. He did not know what, but lately things had been too calm and that was never a good sign.

Then Lord be, here it come, down the street, a wagon pulled by two dark bay horses, driven by two of the Dunn Brothers with the other three as outriders. Now what were they hauling this time? More stolen beef no doubt.

He waited.

They pulled up in front and Bill set the brake.

"Got something for you," Bill said, grinning through his filthy beard.

"And what might that be, some more range beeves you've slaughtered?"

"Well, it's beef all right, but not the four-legged variety," Dal chimed in, still feeling quite good about putting an end to Bitter Creek Newcomb, figuring he'd use some of the money to buy Rose a pretty new dress and maybe a parasol.

Canton swallowed, stood up, and came over to look in the wagon.

"Jesus Christ, is that Bitter Creek Newcomb?"

"And a bonus, Charlie Pierce," Bill said, climbing down and coming to stand next to the lawman.

"I do believe there is a fair amount of reward money on these two and we're here to collect."

Flies were already buzzing the wounds, eating the blood.

"Now that's a pretty sight to you, I bet, ain't it?" Dal said.

"Take 'em over to the undertaker and I'll file the paperwork," Canton said.

Bill nodded at Dal and Dal took the reins and drove the wagon up the street to the undertaker.

"You know where to find us when that money gets approved," Bill said.

Canton watched them go down the street to their butcher shop casual as cats. He wiped sweat from his brow, thinking, *Two more dead and about five that ought to be.*

CHAPTER 26

Tilghman was all smiles, like a coon eating briars, he was when he came to see me.

"What the hell you so chipper about?" I asked.

"I wanted to tell you before you read about it," he said, looking about. "Don't suppose you'd have any more of that coffee with the sipping whiskey in it."

"Why it's not even noon yet and a Sunday to boot."

"I reckon Jesus wasn't opposed to drinking a little, was he?"

"Wine," I said.

"Well that was in his time, this is in mine."

I went and got him the libation and we sat out on the porch and he dawdled in telling me whatever it was had made him fidgety as a kid trying to open his present on Christmas.

"Well . . ." I finally said. "Just what is it you come to tell me? If it's about Bitter Creek Newcomb and Charlie Pierce getting themselves slain by the Dunn Brothers, I already know."

"No," he said taking his sweet time, enjoying every minute of whatever it was tickling his innards.

"Then what, damn it, I ain't got all day to be sitting around trying to guess what you come for."

"You're getting irascible in your old age, Heck," he said.

"I noticed you're wearing a brand new pair of fancy boots," I said. "Kinda feminine with them roses stitched into the shafts. That what it is, you got yourself a new pair of lady boots?"

He looked down at his boots, smiled all the more.

"I caught Doolin," he said.

"Caught him? Where? When?"

"In a bath house in Eureka Springs," he said, now acting casual, as though it were nothing—capturing Bill Doolin, a man whom it seemed like we'd been chasing all our natural-born lives.

"Last I heard he was hiding out down in New Mexico somewhere," I said.

"Might have been, can't say to that."

"Did you have to kill him?"

"No, sir. He went meek as a child once I pointed my six-shooter at him."

"Just like that?"

"Just like that."

He sipped his coffee, obviously enjoying it more than a man should, telling me how he'd captured Doolin, more than the coffee.

"What were you doing in a bath house?"

"Well, to tell the truth, I had a dream that's where I'd catch Doolin," he said.

"You pulling my leg?"

"Maybe." His grin got wider.

"So you just walked in and pointed your pea shooter and he gave up?"

"Pretty much so. I saw him sitting in a lounge reading a newspaper. All I had on me was a towel wrapped around my middle. Hell, he even looked up and right at me and I figured that's it, we're going to have to go to fist fighting. But he just went back to reading his paper. I went on out and found me a pair of trousers and a gun and came back in and said, 'Bill, you've run out of road to run. Put up your hands and don't make this get bloody.

"He sort of shrugged and said, 'All right then.'

"I carried him on up to Stillwater for arraignment and he told me on the way up there he'd plead guilty to murder charges for the shootout at Ingalls in exchange for a fifty-year prison sentence. But when

he went before the judge he pleaded not guilty. I was ordered to take him to the jail in Guthrie. I asked him on the way why he'd changed his mind."

"What'd he say to that?" I asked.

"Said fifty years was a mighty long time."

"Well damn, Bill, I do believe we're finally putting this bad bunch to bed once and for all. Glad you caught him, but I wished it had been me."

"Now you know why I'm wearing these fancy boots," he said. "Reward money."

It was a nice deal, learning Bill had caught Doolin and I went to bed that night feeling a lot better than I had when I got up that morning.

A good ending to a notorious outlaw's journey. Except that it wasn't. Hell, Doolin wasn't locked up two months before he and a bunch of others broke jail.

I phoned Tilghman soon as I heard the news.

He sounded glum.

"Looks like I'm going to have to take these new boots back for a refund," he said.

"Looks like," I said.

"Son of a bitch," he said. "Why can't he stay caught?"

"Or . . ."

"Or that," he said.

The Dane called right after, said, "You hear about Doolin?"

I told him I had. He said he wondered if Tilghman had heard, said, "I bet he's sick at heart."

"No," I said. "Except for those lady boots."

"Huh?" he said.

"Nothing," I said.

I told my Mattie to pack me a kit, that I'd be leaving out again. She wanted to know where. I told her after Bill Doolin and the others who were still on the run.

"Why I thought Bill Doolin was in prison," she said.

"Was," I said. "Ain't no more."

She merely shook her head and gave me the sad eyes.

I told her not to worry. She said, "Don't be a fool. How is a lawman's wife not supposed to worry every time he walks out that door?"

I tried to reassure her the best way I could that nothing was going to keep me from coming home again.

"All that sweet sugar," I said.

She called me a rascal and said she wouldn't kick me out of bed for eating crackers. I laughed. She laughed. I left in the morning.

CHAPTER 27

"We're in a hell of a fix now, ain't we, Bill?" Dynamite Dick Clifton said. "How'd they catch you?"

"Taking a cure at the baths in Eureka Springs."

"Still ailing, was you?"

"All over. Me and Edith had gone down to New Mexico for a spell, but I got to hurting so bad I come back. That and she wanted to be close to her daddy again. He's dying. Got the cancer."

"How long they give you, Bill?"

"Fifty damn years."

Dynamite Dick whistled; his teeth were sharp and crooked as a squirrel's and it made him whistle good. He could whistle "The Girl I Left Behind Me" and "I'll Take You Home Again Kathleen."

"What'd they give you?" Bill asked, fashioning himself a shuck while he sat on a bunk in an area they called the Bull Pen, which contained half a dozen other men.

"I got the same," Dick said. "Figured we must have all been in on the killing of those laws in Ingalls that time."

"Can't hardly blame 'em for thinking that," Bill said. "Since none of us had our names written on the bullets so's they could tell who shot who."

"I think Arkansas Tom got most of 'em. Maybe I got one or two."

"Does it matter?"

"No, I reckon it don't."

They'd been incarcerated nearly a month in the cell, some of the men incarcerated that long and longer. The room stunk of sweat and other body odors and the slops buckets that weren't emptied but once a day. Stunk of tobacco and bad breath and hatred.

Then one day Dick sidled up to Doolin and whispered low, "See that big nigger buck standing over there?"

Bill looked at a man slouched up against the bars, only he didn't look full-blown colored, he looked part Indian too.

"What about him?" Bill asked.

"He's going to grab the guard next time he comes around with the water bucket. Grab him and pin him while some of us others get his gun and keys. You ready to get out of this hell hole?"

Doolin glanced again at the man. He looked dangerous enough, muscular and larger than any other man in the cell. And as if to sense Doolin looking at him, George Lane cut his gaze sharply to Doolin and held it there as if to say, "What the hell you looking at?"

Lane was one of those bad men of mixed blood with none to call his own and hated by everybody and hated everybody in return. There were not many crimes he had not put his hand to.

"Yeah, I'm ready," Doolin said. "What you all want me to do?"

"Just be ready to help out once that coon gets his hands on the guard, then get ready to scat."

So they waited.

And as if ordained, the buck did as he said he would and called the guard closer to the bars, saying he surely wanted a drink of water, said it real nice, nonthreatening. Had gone out of his way since he'd gotten tossed in the Bull Pen to make like he could be your friend, even if you were his jailer. Sweet as a slice of potato pie.

"I bet you want a drink before all these white men spit in it, huh?" the jailer joked and held the bucket out with the dipper handle leaning up.

That's when Lane grabbed the fellow by the throat, struck quick as a rattler, and that big powerful hand grabbed hold and squeezed at the same time, pulling the guard up to the bars.

"Grab his damn gun!" the buck seethed.

One of the others grabbed the gun and cocked it as he put the muzzle to the guard's temple, knocking off his blue-billed cap as he did.

"You hand back them keys real slow or you'll not go home to supper tonight, copper."

The guard's face was turning a deep purple and he gasped and fought to free the strong hand around his throat.

"Ease up or you'll choke that man to death," Doolin said.

"Maybe that's what I aim to do," George Lane said, his eyes red with long-held anger.

"Then we'll never get out of here and they'll hang you."

"Shit, I'm already gone a hang."

"Yeah, well, I thought you wanted to get the hell out of here."

Lane relaxed his fingers and the guard gasped for air like a fish out of water.

"Last time I'm telling you," the prisoner with the gun said. "Hand back them damn keys!"

The guard unclipped them from behind his belt and handed them through to Dynamite Dick who took them and unlocked the door as if he'd been doing it all his life and swung it open. The men rushed out as the buck pulled the guard inside the cell and hit him a crack-hard shot against the jaw that knocked him cold as a brick.

It didn't take long for the lot of them to disappear into the night.

Doolin and Dick followed the railroad tracks north, the steel rails gleaming in the partial moonlight like ropes of silver. They kept going until dawn when they hid down in some timber.

"Which way you think the rest went?" Dick said as he laid down in some tall weeds.

"Don't know and don't care," Doolin said wearily. "I'm just glad we made it out."

They slept the sleep of dead men and hid out all day in the weeds, keeping a watchful eye out for any pursuers. Once they heard dogs barking and baying and figured they were bloodhounds run by prison guards out for them. But then the sound moved off in some other direction until there was just the wind breathing through the weeds and the hum of honey bees in among some clover and worrying the purple thorny heads of bull thistles.

They grew hungry and thirsty and drank fetid water from a ditch then slept some more and whiled away the day until evening came and got up and continued to follow the railroad tracks.

Two or three days of travelling like that, they finally came to the banks of the Cimarron River.

"Well, she's too wide and deep to cross," Dick stated the obvious.

"I know of a ferryman not too far up yonder aways," Doolin said. "I can get him to take us over."

"You think you can trust anybody with the money we got on our heads?"

"I can trust this old boy."

"Why is that, Bill?"

" 'Cause he knows I'll kill him if he says anything."

"Well, that sure would make me think twice," Dick said, whistling sharp through his squirrel teeth.

"We'll go up that way and wait till morning and make sure ain't nobody else but him around."

"I reckon."

The ferryman stood at the edge of the river wearing naught but a pair of faded coveralls and a frayed straw hat watching the sun rise in the east and waiting for his first fares of the day. He lived nearby in a small shack by himself. A wife had run off on him several years back with a fellow the ferryman had sold her to for an hour's pleasure. It was a hard life to earn a living anywhere in the territory less you ran whiskey or robbed banks.

Her name was Renalta and she was French with those hot-blooded ways, dark as a damn Cajun. He'd pulled her out of a cathouse in Tahlequah, paid her pimp sixty damn hard-earned dollars. Needed a housekeeper and cook as much as anything. She seemed eager at first to take on wifely duties. All kinds. But she proved damn quarrelsome too and refused to cook and clean, preferring to laze about and dream. He told her she'd have to earn her keep one way or the other and might as well be doing something she was used to and good at. She agreed. She liked the work better than washing a dish or sweeping a floor.

The fella she ran off with was an Irish drummer of patent medicines, had him a trained bear to attract the crowds. Told Renalta as they lay abed, "You'd make the perfect Salome. You'll attract twice as many as Bruno will. Especially if I dress you in some exotic costumes."

She liked the idea. They left in the middle of the night. The drummer left the bear. The ferryman shot the bear, skinned it out and tacked its hide to the outer wall, and ate the meat all that long winter. All in all it wasn't a bad trade, he thought.

He was standing there watching the sun rise above the river

into a sky without a single flaw when he heard someone say, "Leo."

He turned around startled.

"Shit, Doolin, where'd you come from?" Then he shifted his eyes to the other fellow with Doolin.

"Don't matter where we came from," Doolin said. "I need you to carry us on over to the other side of the river."

"Well, sure. That's what I do, carry folks back and forth across this mean old river."

"Don't suppose you got anything to eat in that old shack?"

"Had some bear meat smoked out but it's all gone. Might have a corn dodger or two."

"That would do us."

"I'll go and get you some."

Doolin watched him shuffle off toward the shack of a house that sat a good one hundred yards back from the river due to flooding nearly every spring.

Soon as he disappeared inside Doolin jumped aboard the ferry and said, "Come on!"

"You not going to wait till he brings us them corn dodgers?" Dick said, his stomach growling.

"Only thing he's liable to bring us is a goddamn gun."

Doolin was already cranking the handle that drew the ferry toward the far shore.

"I never known that bastard to give anybody nothing, not even a corn dodger. No, he's gone for a gun and me and you is standing here in our altogethers with not so much as a stick to defend ourselves. Help me crank this bastard."

Together they worked like fiends drawing the flatboat across the river, the mud-brown water lapping up over the sides, getting their boots wet.

They were nearly halfway across when they saw the ferryman come running from the house, a shotgun in his hands like he was charging the Yankees at Gettysburg.

"Hurry up!" Doolin warned.

The sight of the shotgun being aimed at them from the shore put extra energy in their arms.

Then "BOOM!" and pellets blew up a spray of river not ten feet behind them. "BOOM!" again and a single pellet caught Dick in the calf and caused him to yelp.

He turned and shook his fist at the ferryman who was breaking open the shotgun and plucking out the spent shells before searching through his coverall pockets for more.

"Goddamn your sorry hide!" he yelled.

Doolin kept cranking but was kind of grinning too.

"You tell him, Dick. Give that old bastard hell for stealing his boat."

"He could have put out my eye," Dick squawked.

By now they were out of range and the shotgun proved useless and they saw the old man jumping up and down and cussing words they couldn't make out.

"He's bound to tell it was us who stole his boat," Dick said.

"Don't matter. He would have shot us both and carried our carcasses to the nearest lawdog and sold us for whatever he could have gotten. This way we're alive and he's even poorer than he was and fuck him."

CHAPTER 28

Albert come the other day, my boy by my first wife, Isabelle, who divorced me and took my children back to Georgia.

I'd not seen him since he was a tad, though I had written to him often enough and he'd written me.

Albert was now a big strapping boy with his mother's eyes but the rest was me all over again. I can't say just how proud of him I was, to see him now a man and doing well by himself. He is well spoken and well groomed, had a quick alertness to him but moves about softly.

It was a big surprise to me to open the door and see him standing there with a kit in his hand.

"Daddy," he said. "I wondered if I might visit a while?"

I choked up. I figured maybe his mother might have poisoned his mind against me, but obviously if she tried, it didn't take.

Mattie greeted him like he was her own, kissed him on his cheeks, which caused him to blush and said he was welcome to stay as long as he wished.

We had a right fine supper that night, Mattie putting on the dog for Albert. Had meats and sauces and mashed potatoes, green beans with onions and bacon cooked in 'em the way I like them. Had two kinds of pies: pecan and pumpkin. She treated him like royalty and said more than once what a handsome young man he was.

"You take after your father," she said.

"Yes'm," he would say in that soft-spoken manner.

He told us he had gone to college for a time but had become bored with studying, though he might return someday.

"I'd just like to be out in the world a bit and see what real life is like."

I said he's sure enough see it here in the Nations, probably more than what he bargained for.

"I've been reading of your exploits, father," he said. "In the newspapers and the Police Gazette. *You and Mr. Madsen and Bill Tilghman. They say you three are responsible for rounding up the whole darn bunch of misbehavers."*

I had to smile at that word, misbehavers.

After supper Albert and I went out onto the porch and smoked cigars and he caught me up on his siblings who had not been so inclined to come and visit me too: Henry, Belle, Mary Jo, and Lovic. He said they were all doing fine and that the girls especially asked after me often and that Henry and Lovic cut out articles whenever they saw my name and pasted them in a scrapbook.

"I sure do miss the lot of you," I said. "I'm so sorry that things didn't work out between your mother and me."

"I know, Daddy. It wasn't anyone's fault. None of us kids blame you."

I asked after his mother, more out of politeness than any real interest, and he said she was getting along fine, had been being sparked for several years now by a local fellow who owned a hardware store. Said the fellow's name was Adelmire. Something like that. Said he was an all right fellow as fellows went but he didn't think Isabelle and him would end up getting hitched, that they were just more or less companions.

Then he asked me about what it was truly like being a lawman and I said it wasn't nearly as glamorous as you might think, but there were times when it damn well stirred the blood.

"I'd like to give it a try, Daddy," he said.

"What, being a deputy?"

"Yes, sir. I just don't feature myself as an indoors type of fellow, sit-

ting behind some desk, toting figures all day."

I said there were lots of other kinds a work a fellow could get into with the right schooling, "Doctoring or maybe dentistry and such."

"It ain't for me," he said. "I always wanted to be you."

I didn't quite know what to say to that.

I wanted to dissuade him such notions, but I knew I'd look like a hypocrite because all my life, ever since I was his age, I wanted to be a lawman and I never regretted the work, not once.

"Well, maybe next time I go out on the scout, you could come along. You know how to shoot?"

"I've been practicing a lot," he said.

I didn't tell him it was one thing to shoot targets and a whole other to shoot someone shooting back. Figured there were certain things you had to learn on your own.

"Well, if your mind's made up, Albert . . ."

"It is."

"Your mother know?"

"I told her as much."

"I bet that put a bee in her bonnet, knowing you were coming to me with such a notion."

"She didn't say nothing."

"All right then."

We sat and watched the evening come down around us. Mattie was inside playing the piano, a nice rendition of "Amazing Grace."

My chest was swelled with a sudden rush of deep and abiding love for those around me.

My prayer that night was please, God, don't let anything happen to Albert in my charge or otherwise.

An old owl hooted somewhere in the dark, a shivering sound, then went silent.

CHAPTER 29

The river, rearwards of them now, Doolin said, "You go on, Dick, I'm heading out."

"You ain't going home to Edith?"

"They'll be watching the place. I'd walk right into their guns I was to go there."

"Where the hell you gone a go then, Bill?"

"New Mexico. I know some fellers down there who will do right by me until things die down. I hate having to leave her behind, but I just can't risk it."

"Well, damn."

"What about you?"

Dick looked about. The land all looked the same, big and empty, a lot of space to get lost in, but could be there was a police around every corner and behind every rock and tree too. Damn territory had become crawling with police, like bedbugs in a hotel.

"Reckon I'll hide out in the Nations, it's what I know best."

"Well, good luck to you, then," Doolin said and offered his hand and Dick shook it.

"I reckon there will come a time when we will meet up again and have us some more good times, eh?"

"I reckon," Bill said. "Do me a favor. If you get up around Ingalls, stop by and tell Edith I'm alive and I'll come for her or send for her soon as I'm able. Can you do that?"

"Yes, sir, I reckon I can."

"All right then."

Dick watched Doolin head off toward a distant stand of hardwoods, called after him, "New Mexico is a damn far piece to walk, Bill."

"I ain't aiming to walk it," Bill called over his shoulder and gave a wave of his hand.

In two days' time he came to the ranch of a man he knew named Arthur, just a little scrub place with a few head of cattle and some horses. Arthur ran whiskey sometimes, like a lot of men in those days, to earn a little extra money. Mostly he was on the up and up. He had a daughter, Sylvie they called her. Plain-looking, with large hands for such a skinny gal.

He strode up to the house and saw the gal milking a cow under a lean-to shed, perched on a three-legged stool, her back to him.

"How you this fine morning, Sylvie?" he said

She started, jerked her head around. She had dull brown hair tied up in pigtails, wore a plain calico dress and brogan shoes.

She squinted at him. Her wide-set eyes weren't so good at distance.

"Who you?" she said.

"Friend of your daddy's. He around?"

"No, he's gone."

"Will he be back soon?"

She continued to stare.

"What you want with him?"

"Just want to talk some business," he said.

"Business? What kind of business?"

"You sure enough ask a lot of questions."

"My pa's business is my business. I keep things going round here. Got no ma to do it."

"That a fact?"

"It is a fact. Well, you might just as well sit yourself in some shade, it's awful hot in the sun."

"You're right about that. You mind I pump myself up a ladle of water?"

"No, I don't mind, go ahead," she said and turned back to her milking while Doolin jacked the hand of the pump there in the yard. He looked about as he drank from the dipper he filled, the water cold and sweet straight out of the ground, the way it should be.

The place was all in disrepair, weeds grown up everywhere. There were some chickens kept enclosed in a six-foot by six-foot cage of chicken wire and pieces of lath for posts. There was a rusting harrow over in a patch of weeds, a busted wagon wheel next to it.

He stood there in the shade of a large sycamore watching the girl milk. She did it expertly and finished quick enough and carried the bucket of milk to a spring house and set it inside. Came back wiping her hands on the skirt of her dress.

"You hungry?" she said.

"My belly feels like my throat's been cut," he said. At this she grinned. She had small teeth, like a baby's teeth.

"Shoot," she said, repeating the phrase, "My belly feels like my throat's been cut. That's a good one. Come on inside."

He followed her in, ducking his head as he entered the low-ceilinged large room. There were two cot beds shoved against opposite walls, a table in the middle, and a stove at the far end.

"I got some stew I could heat up for you," she said. "How'd you know my daddy?"

"Way back," he said, taking a seat in one of the two chairs at the table."

"I thought maybe you come to buy a jug off him."

"No," he said.

"He gets two dollars a jug if you want me to go out and get you one."

"No. I don't have any money no how."

She looked over her shoulder at him as she poked red ambers to life in the stove's belly and got it going again then put in a couple of chunks of hardwood.

"Well, I hope you ain't come to ask for a loan. My old man's as broke as the guvermint."

"No, I didn't come to ask for any money. You mind I smoke?"

"Shoot, no," she said. "Might have a pipe myself while this stew is heating." There was a large black cast iron pot atop one of the stove lids.

They sat and smoked and said little, but all the time she was watchful of him. Then they ate and the stew wasn't bad considering.

"What kind of meat you got in this?" he asked.

"This and that," she said.

It didn't assure him of much—this and that kind of meat without knowing what it was. It had a stringy quality to it.

She scraped off the dishes afterward and they sat outside in chairs they carried out. The sun was settling in beyond some ridges that were blue-green in the hazy light.

"When do you reckon your daddy might return?" he said.

She shrugged, leaned and spat off to the side, and said, "I never know when he returns or when he goes. He's a caution."

"Truth is, I was hoping to borrow a horse," he said, looking over to the corral, which by standards of the rest of the place was a right nice corral. There were five horses in it, two of them standing head to hip and the others just standing and staring off like they wanted to be someplace only horses knew about.

"Horse?" she said. "Why I doubt he'd lend you any horse. How would you get it back to him?"

"There's ways," he said.

"Like what?"

"Well I could ride it back. I could send it back on a train."

She laughed and laughed.

"Lord be."

"What's so funny?" he said.

"Well, if you was to ride it back you'd be in the same fix you are now—afoot, in need of a horse. That wouldn't make no sense. And I doubt they'd sell you a train ticket for a horse."

She shook her head in bemused amazement at this man.

Then: "You sure enough are a handsome devil. You want a turn with me afore my daddy gets back?"

"Well, it's generous of you to offer," he said. "But I'm married and trying to get home to my wife."

"Well shoot, where's she at now?"

"A goodly distance from here."

"So you need to borry a horse to go see your wife?"

"Yes, something like that."

"You know, I have a idea."

"What's that?"

"I could let you steal a horse. That way you wouldn't have to worry about bringing it back."

"Steal it?"

"What, you ain't never stole a horse afore?"

"You mean you'd just let me take one of those horses, steal it?"

"Could be, but you'd have to do something for me first."

"Take a turn with you?"

"Lord," she gawped, "you're not only devil good-looking but you're quick in the brains too. What'll you say?"

"Sounds like a right good plan."

"Then let's go afore my pa gets back. He'd probably kill you he caught you diddling me."

"No doubt. Go on in and get yourself ready. I'll just wash up a bit at the pump."

She ran inside.

God, he thought.

Later when he rode off, she was still tied to the bed screaming, "You pie-eyed bastard, leaving me like this and not even keeping your end of the deal. Why, you dirty son of a bitch! Daddy! Daddy!"

Well, he thought with a smile, it's what she said she wanted, to be tied up and have him do things to her. But tying is as far as he could stand it.

She'd asked him what his name was as he was tying the knots.

"Bitter Creek Newcomb," he said, thinking his dear dead friend would not mind the lie.

The last thing she said before she realized things weren't going to work out the way she thought they were was, "Bitter Creek Newcomb, why I heard of you. I heard you was a real ladies' man."

"Yes'm. That's what I hear."

He surely hoped her daddy wouldn't be overly long gone and would come home soon enough and untie the poor thing. And he thought it was damn decent of him to put an old hat he found hanging on a peg over her flower of sex for modesty's sake.

You are a gentleman tried and true, Bill Doolin.

Chapter 30

Doolin's whereabouts had become a mystery once more. Nobody had reported him in all the territory. I knew it wasn't just us U.S. deputy marshals on the scout, that every sort of bounty hunter and Pinkerton Detective was also looking for him and those others who broke jail in Guthrie. There was a passel of reward money if you toted it all up.

Time me and Albert hit the town, you couldn't scrape a sliver of new information with a paring knife.

We headed to near Lawson where Doolin was known to have kept a place with his wife, Albert asking me all about Doolin as we went.

"What sort of fellow is he?"

"He ain't bad," I said, "if you don't count his crimes, the murders he's committed, and so forth. Personally I knew him before he got into the crime business and he was all right, not hard like a lot of these boys who thieve and rob and murder."

I told him by example about the Rufus Buck gang who'd not only murdered but raped white women and what a bad bunch of killers they were.

"They killed everything they came across that walked or talked," I said. "Now Bill Doolin wasn't anything like that. Probably could have been a preacher or a shop owner."

"What is it you think causes men to go bad like that?" Albert asked.

We were sauntering along at a walk and I was smoking my pipe, real leisurely like, enjoying the company of my son, our precious time together.

"Well, it's hard to say, Albert. Any number of things will affect a man's mind, easy money, loose women, a life that don't call for regular steady work like most of us do."

"But the same could be said of lawmen, couldn't it—that part of not calling for steady work at least?"

"True enough, boy. And maybe us lawdogs are sometimes self-righteous, but we are righteous enough."

"What about you?" he asked. "You ever tempted to cross over the line?"

"No. Never was. I like sleeping at night without having to worry about getting arrested and clapped in the jail. Something sweet to be said about freedom. Wouldn't be nothing in God's world would make me do anything to spend even one night in jail."

"It must not worry fellows like Doolin," he opined.

"Oh, I think it worries 'em all right, they just don't see no way to get out of the life they've made. It's too late. One way or the other they'll either get locked up or get killed by fellows like me and you, now that you want to become a lawman."

We rode on silent till we reached outside of Ingalls and the clapboard house that was Doolin's residence. I told Albert to remain seated on his horse but have his Winchester ready just in case and I walked up and knocked on the door.

A slightly handsome woman with russet hair pinned into a bun and demurely dressed in gingham answered the door. Clinging to her skirts was a small boy, Doolin's I guessed. Cute little fellow.

"Yes, can I help you?" she said.

I announced myself and what I'd come for. She looked past my shoulder at Albert mounted, his Winchester balanced on his thigh.

"I've not seen my husband in months," she said.

I told her I didn't aim to kill him if I didn't have to, but that it did not mean that any number of other armed men might not feel the same way.

"You'd be doing your husband a favor if you told me where he *was and let me try and arrest him alive," I said.*

She winced at this.

"If I knew, I'd tell you, Officer Thomas. I don't want to see him murdered."

"No, ma'am, I reckon you don't. Neither do I."

"Well, he's not here," she said, "and I've no idea where he might be."

I wrote down my telephone number and asked that she call and leave a message if I wasn't there if she heard from Bill.

"I've no telephone, sir."

"Well, there's probably one in town somewhere, I'd imagine. Or, if not, just send a wire."

She merely nodded and closed the door.

Albert was eager to know what I'd found out.

"Nothing," I said. "Nor did I expect to."

"You believe her?"

"I do. I think she loves him enough to turn him in rather than see him killed. I sure do feel sorry for that little fellow of theirs."

We rode on with no idea how long or if or when we might find Doolin. And I truly did hope we could take him alive when we did find him, but was also truly aware I might have to put a bullet through his heart.

Chapter 31

Little Dick West had figured never to see none of the Oklahombres again. Settled as he was in an encampment in North East, New México, just him and three harlots he referred to as "sisters."

He was idly watching the sisters bathe in a creek that ran near the old cabin, the sisters frolicking like wood nymphs much to Little Dick's pleasure. It surely was something to see them slick as cavorting seals, the water sheeting off their bare skin, their hair wet as kelp, and though they were as ugly as mud hens, they still offered a great degree of pleasure to a man as lonely and hid out as Little Dick West.

By his side was a Winchester rifle and in his belt, two revolvers, a Colt peacemaker and a Welby English bulldog revolver. Dick was not one to take chances of going about unarmed; too many lawmen who could use the reward money roved about.

The sisters were bare-assed and chunky and Little Dick leaned propped up on one elbow trying to decide which of the three he would take to his bed this evening. He sort of favored the black-haired one, Della, over the other two; she could tell the damndest stories that kept him laughing.

So it was on Della he was concentrating most when he espied a lone rider headed his way.

"You gals climb out of that water and run to the house, someone's a coming."

They hopped to, because Dick could be a caution to deal

with when you didn't obey him.

He stood and took up his rifle and put it to his shoulder and held it steady as he sighted down the length of the barrel, putting the iron front sights on the rider who was coming on at a good pace. His finger rested on the curve of the trigger.

He held that way until he could see it was a man acted more like he was running from something rather than running to something.

"Why shit, it's ol' Bill Doolin," he muttered when the rider came near enough, and lowered his rifle.

Bill pulled up and sat there.

"Little Dick, you haven't turned into a lawdog since I seen you last, have you?"

"Are you crazy?"

Doolin smiled through his bushy black beard.

"Where you hailing from and how close is the laws on your ass?"

"Broke jail in Guthrie and I doubt there is any laws smart enough to track me this far. I've checked my back trail every twenty miles or so and the only thing following was a crow once and the sun."

"Well, climb on down and put up your cayuse."

"Will do, gladly," Doolin said and slipped from the saddle, glad to be relieved of the pounding ride. He led the horse over to the stream and let it drink then unsaddled it and led it over to the brush corral where Little Dick kept a pair of matched bays and turned it out.

"That's a right pert horse," Little Dick said with the same appraising eye he had for womanly flesh.

"Borrowed it," Doolin said. "Need to figure out how to return it."

"Borrowed, huh?"

"You got any grub a fellow could eat?"

"Sure, sure, I'll have the sisters make you up a plate."

"Sisters?"

"What I call my inamoratas," Dick said with glowing smugness and called them from the house. They came out dressed in thin shifts that barely contained their heavy bosoms, still giggling.

"Lord a mercy," Doolin said. "Where'd you come by such?"

"Oh, killed a fellow over near Sunrise for them. A whore man, he was. Come up on them and he was beating them there in the middle of the road like stubborn mules. I asked him to leave off and he told me to mind my own goddamn business and I told him that a man beating the hell out of women folk was my business and he told me they weren't women folk but goddamn whores and his whores to boot and continued to whip at 'em with a buggy whip.

"I pulled my piece and said he had one more chance to leave off and he come at me cutting that whip through the air and I shot him in the face. Well, they was all scared and crying by then and I said they ought to come along with me. And of course they took his cash money for their troubles and I tied my horse to the back of his rig and off we come. Been living with me ever since."

"That's a hell of a story you tell, Dick. But is any of it true?"

Dick simply smiled and said, "Maybe."

He had them fix a plate of victuals, beans and sowbelly and cornbread. Said, "Susie here is the cook, and Lenetta yonder is the housekeeper and Della yonder, well, Della's a sort of jack of all trades, if you get my drift."

"I see," Bill said, sopping a piece of cornbread in the bean's soup. "Looks like you've done well for yourself since leaving the territory."

"Done all right, can't complain."

Doolin reached in his pocket and took out a fold of money

and peeled off several bills and held it forth to Dick.

"What's that for?"

"Need to lay low here for a while if you can stand me."

" 'Course I can stand you, but ain't no need to offer me money."

"Buy the sisters something pretty with it, maybe more victuals."

"Ah, you know I can't take your money, Bill."

"Hell, go ahead. I'm doing all right."

Later that evening the two men sat out under the stars smoking while the sisters busied themselves within the cabin.

"Most of the boys are dead or arrested," Doolin said and ticked off the names.

"Bitter Creek?" Dick said.

"Figured you might not have heard about it way down here in this outcountry."

"Who was it got him?"

"You remember that little darling he shacked with?"

"Rose? Hell she'd be hard not to remember. Sweet as a piece of hard candy."

"Well, it was her brothers laid him low. Him and Charlie Pierce. Shot 'em down like dogs. Done it for the reward money."

"Jesus, they did that to their own sister's sweetheart?"

Doolin nodded.

"They got Dalton too."

"Bill? Who was it?"

"The laws."

"Anybody else?"

"Shit, I reckon. They're killing each other all over the Nations, the laws and men like us."

"I'm glad I got out when I did or I might be under the sod myself."

For several moments there was just quiet contemplation as the night came down around them, naught but the sound of the sisters inside giggling and chatting with one another, the rattle of dishes being put away and later the clack of dominoes being played on the kitchen table.

"Them gals is crazy for dominoes," Little Dick said after a bit puffing his pipestem.

More silence as Bill seemed lost in reverie of missing things.

As if to read his mind, Dick said, "How's Edith?"

"I think she's all right," Doolin said fashioning yet another cigarette. "We got us a son now."

"Well, say, that is good news."

"Yes but . . ."

Doolin let his thoughts trail off. It was too painful to think of his family so far away and him forced on the run.

"I reckon you're missing her bad?" Dick said.

"I am indeed. You got a match I could use?"

Little Dick handed him a Blue Diamond match from a box he had taken from inside the house that sat on a shelf by the stove.

Bill struck it till the head shot into flame and cupped it to the end of his cigarette then snapped it out and tossed it away.

"Say listen," Dick said. "You want you can spend the night with one of the sisters if you're lonely."

"No insult intended," Bill said. "But I ain't that lonely yet."

Both of them chuckled and let the night come on as it would, their reverie spoiled only later by the yip-yip of a coyote calling to its mate, a call that was not answered and Bill reckoned he knew how the coyote felt.

CHAPTER 32

Edith Doolin grows lonely in her abode. From a back bedroom she hears her dying father's ragged breathing, has called for a doctor to come to the house but thus far no doctor has arrived. She fears that outsiders are fearful of coming to the house knowing that the laws are on the scout for Bill; the fear of strangers is they might be mistaken for her husband and gunned down without a chance. There is a thirty-thousand-dollar reward on his head, enough to make trigger fingers itchy.

She has heard too that it is not just the laws who are looking for Doolin, but bounty hunters. The Dunn Brothers, for one.

She has met Rose Dunn, a comely young woman who wears daisies in her hair and acts often a bit odd, silly as a child, which she is, given her age.

Rose had once come to bring a message to Bill on behalf of Bitter Creek Newcomb, saying, "Howdy, I'm Rose, where is your man?"

Edith felt her innards clench, not sure who the girl was at first, fearful she may have come with news that she was pregnant with Bill's child, or the like.

But instead Rose Dunn had held a piece of paper with penciled scribbling on it that was barely legible, written in the hand of George Newcomb himself and signed, *Bitter Creek.*

The note was asking that Bill come, that he had bunged up his knee and was unable to ride but that he had something he wanted to discuss that "was vry impotant."

"Why Bill's gone to town," Edith said. "But I'll be glad to give this to him upon his return."

The girl was unkempt, but still Edith could see her allure for most men: those doe eyes and pouting mouth. She had a sexuality that most women could only hope for, a sexuality that was as natural as rain or wind through the trees or stars at night. She did not need to try, Edith was sure, to seduce men, but rather allow herself only to be seduced by them.

She'd invited the girl to stay for dinner and Rose had readily accepted and commented as she ate on Edith's glass birds that lined the sill of her kitchen window.

"Them is some pretties," she said. "Where'd you get them? I'd like to get myself some."

Edith explained that they were heirlooms handed down by her mother.

The term seemed to confuse the girl.

"Hair looms?"

"No, heir," Edith enunciated, to which Rose nodded as if she understood the difference.

"Tell me, child, how it was you came to become friends with Bitter Creek? He seems so much older than you."

The girl stared up at her from her plate of victuals with those large luminous brown eyes in a curious manner.

"Oh, well, yes, George is old enough to be my pa." Then she giggled. "But I sure don't think of him as my daddy, if'n that's what you mean."

"No, I didn't mean to imply anything of the sort," Edith said, feeling the flush of embarrassment rise in her cheeks.

"I guess it was just that George liked me and I liked him and he's always been sweet to me, calls me his 'Baby Doll.' "

The girl ate without bothering to wash her face or hands and Edith thought it too presumptive to request that she do so. She ate quickly until the fork scraped the china plate.

"Well," she said. "I got to get on, ma'am. You be sure and give Bill Doolin that note, won't you? George'd be awfully mad he wasn't to get it. He's been waiting, laid up with a bum knee."

"I will," Edith said and watched the girl ride off on a small sorrel horse with a roached mane, its tail braided with small ribbons tied in it.

And now Edith wondered thinking back on what she knew of George and Rose and George's death at the hands of her brothers, if the Dunn boys might be waylaying for Bill like they had George.

It was hard to believe that they would kill their sister's sweetheart, a man who was nearly one of their own in every way. Now that Bill had confessed the truth of his "cattle" operations, she knew that Newcomb had been part of it, knew him to be a hardcase just like those Dunn boys. Seemed there was no such thing as honor among thieves.

God, she thought, and peered out the windows to see if she could spot anyone out there hiding with a gun.

Her father coughed and called her name.

His room smelled of a waning of the flesh. He held forth his hand toward her, his skeletal fingers quavering.

"Come," he whispered.

She drew a chair up next to the bed and held his hand.

He cut his pale watery gaze to her.

"Will you be all right?" he said.

"Of course," she said bravely.

"I don't know which one of us will go first, Bill or me," he said.

She closed her eyes so tightly they hurt, blinked back tears that were welling and wanted to break free.

"Why do you say such things, Father?"

"Because . . . it's true . . ."

"Oh, Daddy . . ."

She patted his hand. It was warm and thin-boned.

"Have you heard from . . . him?" he rasped.

"Nothing lately," she said.

"Daughter, there are . . . there are other men . . . better men. Don't forget that."

She no longer was able to hold back the tears and they slid down her overly warm cheeks.

"Hush now," she whispered. "Get some sleep."

The boy roused in another room. He had been napping. He called, "Mama. Mama."

"Yes," she replied. "I'm coming."

"Mama. Mama."

She rose and went to him and what she saw in that still too young and innocent face was traces of her husband. No matter what happened, she would have the boy to remind her.

The boy reached his small arms toward her and she picked him up and held the weight of him on one hip and he snuggled his small delicate face against hers.

God, what would she do without Bill.

CHAPTER 33

Having had no good luck in locating Doolin, Albert and I rode over to visit Bill Tilghman to see if he might have any further news on our lost duck. Tilghman was his usual jocular self but with a huge bandage on his right ear that caused his head to look off kilter.

I introduced him to Albert and he couldn't believe the size of him since the last they met Albert was a tadpole.

"Lord, look at you, Albert."

Albert simply blushed at the attention. Tilghman invited us in to the front parlor of his place.

"Wife's off shopping for calico cloth," he said. "How you boys fixed for something to drink or eat?"

I said we were fine on that account and asked him what happened to his ear.

He touched the bandage and grinned like some old coon eating corn on the cob.

"I had me a hell of a run against some real desperados," he said. Then laughed like a madman.

Me and Albert just looked at each other.

When Bill caught his breath he fired up his meerschaum, puffed it two or three times contemplative-like, keeping the suspense alive.

"You heard of them two gals, the ones they call Cattle Annie and Little Britches?"

"Sure," I said. "Supposed to have been spies for Doolin's gang."

"Well, I heard that, when they wasn't selling whiskey to the Indians and sticking up grocery stores."

Albert said, "That was their real names, Cattle Annie and Little Britches?"

Bill exhaled a cloud of tobacco smoke that hung in the air and said, "No, son, ain't hardly nobody uses real names out here if they don't have to, especially if they are on the dodge or otherwise consider themselves some sort of bad hombres.

"Their real names are Jennie Stevens and Anna McDoulet, but hell, that don't sound near as romantic as Cattle Annie and Little Britches, does it?"

Albert said he reckoned not.

"I'm going to die of old age before you get around to telling me what any of this has to do with your bandaged ear," I said. I guess I was growing grumpy in my elder years—that and not being able to run Doolin to ground.

"Just a sec," Bill said. "I need to refresh my Arbuckle with some of what I got out in the kitchen way back up under the cupboard where the Missus can't find it."

Me and Albert waited there in the sunlit parlor with its tall floor-to-ceiling windows and tatted curtains.

"He's quite a character, Mr. Tilghman is," Albert opined.

"Always has been and probably always will be."

"This is some house too."

"Ought to be," I said. "Bill collects more reward money than me and Chris combined."

Bill rejoined up and settled back into his rocking chair, his forefinger hooked in the handle of a china coffee cup decorated with blue flowers.

"Now where was I?" he said, knowing full well where he was.

"At the point where I just turned ninety years old waiting for you to tell me some tale about some girl children who've become the scourge of the Nations," I said.

"Your daddy has gotten awfully cranking, ain't he, son?" Bill said to Albert. Albert did not reply.

"Well, anyway, as I was saying, those two delinquents half took up with the Doolin gang—Annie going so far as to hitch her star to Red Buck Weightman till he cleared the territory and went to Texas—doth continued their petty crimes, and not so petty until Sheriff Frank Lake caught Little Britches."

"What about Annie?" Albert foolishly asked.

Bill shook his head as if he'd just saw a frog fly.

"Didn't catch her, just Little Britches."

I offered a long hard sigh to indicate my displeasure with the slowness of this wounded-ear mystery. Bill cut his mischievous gaze my way and continued.

"So, anyway, Sheriff Lake has her caught and arrested and soon as they hit Pawnee she begs him for a meal, bawling and crying how hungry she is and how she ain't eat in three or four days and he feels sorry for her and takes her into a café and orders her a meal, which she hurriedly consumes, and then while he's paying the freight she bolts out the back door and steals a horse and rides off into the night."

Tilghman snapped his fingers and laughs around the stem of his pipe as if enjoying this.

"But you want to know the real kicker?" he said without waiting for an answer. "It was town marshal Canton's horse she stole!"

His laughter was uproarious until it turned into a coughing jag. His face grew as purple as a garden beet.

I waited until he stopped entertaining himself and no doubt Albert, then said, "Okay, but we still ain't got to that part about your ear. Will we ever or were you holding off till another day?"

"Oh, hold your damn horses, Heck. I'm coming to it."

"That's some story, Marshal Tilghman."

"So, anyway," Bill continued after taking a healthy swallow of his popskull coffee, "Me and Steve Burke give chase and tracked her down to her hideout where she has rejoined her girlfriend, Annie, and they started tossing lead at us like bona fide outlaws.

"Burke says to me, 'Bill, I ain't sure I can shoot no woman.' I say, Steve, them ain't women, they're just girls."

Again, a fit of laughter. The son of a bitch is really enjoying his story, as usual.

"A'fore you know it, they're making another run of it and I tell Burke to go after one and I'll go after the other. He ends up catching Annie, though she fights him like a hellion and scratches him all to hell before he got the irons on her.

"In the meantime I'm riding hell bent for leather after Britches and she's on some sort of goddamn racer it seems to me and I know I'm never going to catch that animal and thus her. So I haul up short, jump out of my saddle, take aim, and drop that stud, sending that youngster tumbling ass over teakettle."

"I bet she didn't care a damn about you shooting her horse," I said.

"Oh, Lord, you'd a thought I killed her mama the way she carried on," Bill said. "Anyway, I didn't realize till later on that I was bleeding, that one of her shots had clipped my ear. She said she wished it had been an inch to the right and would have blown out my brains. Talk about some folks what got hard in such few years of living, it was them two."

"What happened to them, Mr. Tilghman?" Albert asked.

"Oh, they both got sent away to reformatory in Framingham, Massachusetts," Bill said with a degree of satisfaction. "Teach them not to mess with gun toughs like me."

He just couldn't help himself.

"Well, that's one hell of a tale, Bill," I said. "How much reward money did you collect on that dangerous mission?"

"Shit, less than a hundred dollars, me and Burke. Hardly worth the chase. Cost me three dollars to get my ear patched and my wife said I look ugly with half an ear—that it don't match my other one."

"Hell, you always did look ugly," I said.

He said, "Shit, think I'll have me another pick-me-up before the

Missus gets back from her shopping. You sure you won't join me?"

"You know I'm pretty much a teetotaler anymore."

"I know it. I still don't know how you ever owned a saloon once without ending up an alky."

Albert looked at me.

"I'll have to tell you about it sometime," I said. "But seems like we've had enough tall tales for one day."

Chapter 34

Days turned into weeks of sitting around, playing dominoes, watching the sisters cavort in various states of undress, but Doolin had no interest in these unhandsome nymphets. Little Dick was drunk most of the time, slovenly, lust-filled, athwart as a man could get.

Occasionally a rider or two would stop by and buy a hot meal, a bottle of whiskey Little Dick would tap from one of several barrels. They'd also usually buy a turn with one of the bawds, which generally led to a lot of hooting and hollering of which Little Dick took great pleasure.

"The more them boys enjoy themselves the more money I can put in my tin box," he'd say.

"I never thought I'd see the day you turned into a pimp," Doolin said regrettably. When he'd first met Little Dick years earlier they were both working hands on Oscar Hasell's ranch in Logan, O.T. Little Dick was a wet-behind-the-ears preacher's kid who'd run away from his home in Texas, said his old man whipped him like a government mule.

"He'd only do it when he got drunk," Dick related in the early days of their meeting as cowboys. "Trouble was he was hardly ever not drunk. He went after my mother too and I finally had had enough of it and busted him across the head with a whiskey bottle. Thought it would break into pieces, but it did not. Just clanged off the old man's head like it was made of iron."

"The bottle or the old man's head," Bill had asked. They had been sitting in the shade of a line shack while out looking for strays.

"Both," Dick said. "Goddamn but it gave him the staggers though. He chased me about threatening to drown me in the water tank and I knowed he'd do it too if he caught hold of me."

"Jesus," Doolin said rolling himself a shuck as he listened.

"I never seen such an evil son of a bitch," Dick said.

"What do you think made him that way?"

"I think his old pappy did him the same way he was doing ma and us kids, just beat on them whenever he wasn't happy with something. Again, like his drinking, he was hardly ever happy with anything. Just a miserable old son of a bitch is what he was."

They heard a cow bawling off in the canebrakes and Doolin started to rise but then Dick said, "Ah, let's just rest here a spell in this cool shade a minute longer, that old cow, she ain't going nowhere."

The kid borrowed Doolin's makings and rolled himself a shuck and struck a match of a rusted nail head poking from one of the shack's side boards.

"You ever had yourself a whore?" he said.

"Sure, ain't you?"

For a minute Dick didn't say anything, just sat there smoking like a big shot.

"Well, unlike some who would lie about it," he said, "I ain't ashamed to admit I'm still a virgin."

"Well, they ain't nothing wrong with that," Doolin said. "You're probably better off than half these waddies walking around with the pox, straining to piss and having to take the mercury cure."

"Jesus Christ, I heard about that," Dick said, cringing. "They say they stick a piston needle right up your pecker to put it in."

"A night with Venus is a lifetime with Mercury," Bill chuckled.

"Shit. I reckon when I do get saddlebroke it best be with a good gal and not one of those slatterns in town."

"I ain't mentioning names but there was a fellow worked here up and married himself a gal that ended up giving him the clap, or maybe it was the syphilis—some widow lady."

"Now that'd be some hell of a news to learn, wouldn't it?"

"It sure would."

"Your own wife."

"Damn straight."

Doolin figured he'd take the kid under his wing and help steer him straight. But the first time they hit town on pay day, Dick got his field plowed by a chunky gal with short platinum hair and he blew his entire pay on her over that long cruel weekend.

And sure enough three days later he was straining to piss and cussing every second of it and had to take the mercury cure.

He never did seem to walk right after that, just slightly off kilter.

And now here he was years later a pimp and whiskey peddler and looking twice as old as he was.

And as if to read Doolin's thoughts, Dick sat up of a sudden from where he'd been stretched out on the floor and said, "Say, you remember that time I lost my cherry to that dirty little whore up in Logan?"

Bill went outside for some air. Air that was brittle-hard cold, like as if you were leaned up against iron. Air that roared down off the Sangre de Christos with the fury of a drunken pa and whistled through the aspens.

Oh how he longed to be with Edith, in a warm bed, the two of them lying next to each other. He tried and tried to figure out how he could go straight, right his wrongs, erase his past.

He'd give anything to do it.

He walked around the compound, his fists stuffed down in the pockets of a sheepskin coat, the collar drawn up and his hat pulled down tight over his ears. The horses whinnied in the corral as if to protest the cold, the wind ruffling their manes and tails so that they stood faced away from it.

The outhouse door flapped and banged but Doolin had no urge to go and close it. He'd come to start to hate the place and everything about it. He hated the fact that the laws had chased him away from Edith and his boy—all the family he had.

Little Dick watched from inside, rubbed a circle of frost from the window glass and thought, *What the goddamn hell is he just walking around like that for, in that shitting cold weather?*

Thought, *Doolin ain't the same feller I used to know. Something in him's gone soft. Probably being married's done it to him. Glad as hell I ain't never married. Wouldn't want to be tied down and find myself walking around in the cold pining for a woman. Leastways not when they's any number of women to be had.* Why settle on one, he'd argued with Doolin and other married men he knew.

Doolin had simply said, "You don't understand it till you feel it, what love is."

Now the damn fool was out there just walking in big circles.

By nightfall Doolin had come up with a plan on maybe how to make things right again. It was more wishful thinking than true plan, but he knew he needed to get back to Edith however he could.

He leaned in close to a sheet of foolscap under the glow of an oil lamp and scratched out a message with a nib pen he dipped in a bottle of India ink. His penmanship was never much good so he took his time, writing careful in order that the message be legible.

Dere Heck.
I ben thinkin you ain't never gone run me to ground cause I won't let you. But on the othr hand, you and them others has me in a bind whereas it Is hard to bee with my family. So what I'm willin to do is turn myself in If you can get me amnasty and we can put an end to all this tom foolry. I will lay up my guns and turn strait and stay that way and will sign a paper To that effect. Just let my Edith know if this is possible and I will come quick and turn in my guns.

Y.O.S. Wm Doolin

He blew on the last lines to hasten the ink's drying then carefully folded the letter and laid back on the bed. It felt as though a weight had been lifted from him. If only the law would agree then everything would be all right.

For the first time in several long years he felt like a frozen man touched by sunlight.

Tomorrow he would ride into the post office and mail the letter and then wait to hear from Edith.

From the other rooms he could hear the snores of harlots and Little Dick West and felt no connection to any of them at all.

Chapter 35

To say I was surprised to have gotten Doolin's letter offering to turn himself in if offered amnesty couldn't quite describe it. I called Tilghman and the Dane and told them about it. They said, "Well, that son of a buck sounds like he's worn down to a nubbin, don't it?"

"Yes," I agreed. "But there is no way he will be forgiven for his crimes. I know Judge Parker would never consider it and neither would I."

"We've about worn out his gang and I reckon he doesn't have nobody backing his play no more, either," Tilghman said.

"I reckon not," Madsen agreed. "You going to send back a reply, or just let him stew in his own juices?" asked Tilghman.

"I'm going to offer that he turn himself in with the only promise that I won't shoot him on sight, is what I'm going to offer."

Both of them agreed that Doolin had painted himself into a corner with nowhere to run, that he sounded like a man who'd heard the death bells tolling. I told the others I was going to carry that letter over to his wife and see could she persuade him to give up unless she wanted to see him put on a block of ice.

"You best go armed and with a committee," Madsen suggested. "Hell, he might already have come back there."

I said I'd go prepared and they wished me good luck, Tilghman saying he was leaving out in the morning on the trail of a pair of wanted mixed bloods who'd been kicking up sand around Okmulgee, and Madsen said he had to haul a wagonload of prisoners to Fort Smith, otherwise he'd like to go with me. I said I had Albert along and would get one or two others to go with me.

That evening Albert and me sat and ate supper, one of my favorites that Mattie fixed: chicken fried steak, mashed potatoes and gravy, green beans, and buttermilk, followed by coffee and rhubarb pie.

We ate till we were about to burst.

I saw the look on Mattie's face when I told her we were heading out in the morning and that we would most likely be gone for several days.

"Who is it this time?" she asked.

"Doolin," I said.

Her face grew even more cloudy, her eyes full of concern.

"I went to Madam Drew's today," she said with the most somber expression I'd ever seen on her.

Madam Drew was a fortune teller and Mattie believed in spiritual things.

"Well, now you know how I feel about that," I said.

"She knows things most don't, Heck."

"She knows how to make a buck," I said rather coldly. I didn't want to sound mean but I couldn't really help it. I figured if one person had such gifts to foretell the future, then why didn't we all have them? I thought the woman was a charlatan through and through.

"Oh, Heck," Mattie said with quivering lip. "Why don't you even consider the possibility that there are things going on around us we aren't aware of?"

" 'Cause I don't. I believe in what I can see, touch, taste. If there's such things as ghosts and spirits, how come we all can't see them, just some can?"

She shook her head in distress.

Albert intervened and said, "Daddy, you ought not be so hard on Mattie. She's a right to believe what she wants, just like you do."

"Thank you," whispered Mattie.

"What was it Madam Drew told you?" Albert asked with a

concerned expression to make up for my skeptical one, I supposed.

She turned her moist gaze to him and said softly, "She said I should be careful, that someone in my family was in grave danger and that we all of us ought to remain close to one another for the next two weeks."

I'd had enough and stood away from the table and went outside to smoke a cigar, letting my pipe be.

The night air was clean and cool and silent and up and down the street I could see lights on in houses. We lived far enough away from the main drag where all the action was, the saloons and gambling houses and hurdy-gurdy gals not to be troubled by their noise.

I studied the heavens as I leaned against a porch post and spotted the constellation Orion and then traced the Little Dipper from the handle of the Big Dipper. I wondered how it was sailors learned to read the stars in order to cross the seas. It seemed like such a mystery to me—like foretelling futures. Of all the damn foolishness.

Albert came out after a bit saying how he'd helped Mattie clean up the dishes. He was cut of a different cloth than me in many ways, just as I was of my own father.

"How you doing, Father?"

"Doing fine," I said.

"You can't blame her for worrying over you."

"I don't blame her," I said.

"You think we'll ever run Doolin down?"

I shrugged.

"Me personal? I can't say, but I'd put money on it if I was a betting man. We run the rest of his lot down, pretty much have rubbed them all out. He's bound to slip up sooner or later. They always do."

"Too bad something couldn't be worked out to let him give himself up."

I looked at Albert standing there, a good three inches taller than me already, that passive handsome face that wouldn't hardly grow whiskers yet, still so young and innocent. I was that way once, but so long ago I forgot when.

"In life there are some rivers you don't ever cross and expect there to be a bridge waiting when you return," I said. "Doolin knows that as well as I do."

"Yes, sir," he said.

"You take a life wantonly, you are bound by the laws of man and God to make amends. Without law, what do you have?"

"Nothing, I reckon, sir."

"Might come a time we'll face Doolin down, and knowing what I know of him, he won't just throw up his hands and give up. Thing is, are you willing to pull the trigger if it comes to that?"

He didn't say anything, just stood there staring off into the dark.

"Good night, then," I said and went on inside to leave him be with his thoughts. I found Mattie in our bedroom changing into her night clothes.

"I reckon you'll want to get an early start," she said.

I was tempted to ask at what, but it wasn't any time to be joking around. I could still hear the hurt in her voice.

"I reckon," I said.

"Then come on to bed and get you some sleep."

I undressed and got into the bed next to her and for a long time we laid there in the dark silence and then we heard the front door open and close and Albert's footsteps crossing the floor to his room.

"Heck?"

"Yes, honey, what is it?"

"Don't you go and get that boy killed."

"I won't."

"All right then."

Goddamn Doolin for putting the worry in my wife's heart.

CHAPTER 36

Doolin was saddling his horse by the time Little Dick came out of the cabin tugging his galluses up over his bare skinny shoulders with one hand and scratching his backside with the other.

"You off for a morning ride, Bill?"

"Going home," Bill said.

"Home? Why you think that's a smart move, considering?"

"I think it's all the move I got left, Dick. I miss my family, my wife and boy. It's been too long since I seen them and it looks like Heck ain't never gone answer my offer."

"Offer? What offer is that?"

"I sent a letter off a few weeks back offering to turn myself in and hang up my guns if they'd give me amnesty. Ain't heard so much as a peep back."

"Why, Lord God, Bill, why would those sons a bitches give you amnesty when they can just as easily put a bullet in you and collect the rewards?"

"I don't know, I was just hoping is all. It was my last play to try and get myself straightened around, go back to an honest life. Like what you and me once had, Dick. You remember those days, don't you?"

Dick scratched up in his nest of hair.

"I don't know what I'd want to go back to 'em for," Dick said. "I kinda like the way things are now."

Doolin looked at him across the back of his horse as he

grabbed the belly strap. What he saw was a dead man, maybe two if he could have looked at himself.

"We're about into a whole new century," Bill said, pulling the belly strap up tight. "You ever imagine what that's gone be like? I sort of like the idea of living in two different centuries. I intend on it. Me and Edith and our boy. I'd like to see him grow into manhood and end up some day being proud of his daddy. I got to try, Dick."

"Sure, sure, I understand. But I think if you go back up into the territory you'll just be looking for that bullet with your name on it."

Doolin finished up the saddle then tied his bedroll on behind, his saddle pockets, and slipped his Winchester down in the saddle sock almost like a finality, a punctuation to the discussion. He came around and offered his hand to Little Dick who shook it.

He looked off toward the house and said, "You take care of the Sisters, Dick, or better still, let them take care of you."

Dick grinned slyly.

"I always wanted to be the rooster."

"Well, now you are."

Dick watched Bill fork the saddle horse and turn it out toward the road. He watched until Bill Doolin was nothing more than just a speck against the big blue New Mexican sky, then nothing at all, as if he'd never been, and turned and walked back to the cabin and found him a warm spot in among the sleeping cats and thought as he eased into sleep, *Jeez Christ, Bill, you are going to your grave.*

Chapter 37

The Dunn boys were biding their time with liquor, cards, and stolen beeves. They were surprised to see Ol Frank Canton coming up the street with a couple of fellows, one of whom they did not recognize and the other, the lawman Heck Thomas.

The three men reined in in front of the butcher shop.

They did not bother to dismount and Bee called inside, "Bill, you and Dal might want to come out here."

When the elder brothers appeared, Bill Dunn wiped his bloody fingers against the stained apron covering his middle.

"Looks like half the law in the county has come to visit," he said. "Who's this with you, Heck?"

"That's my son, Albert. Albert," Heck said, turning his head only slightly, "These are the notorious Dunn Brothers, some of them anyway. Men hunters when they ain't stealing and butchering beeves."

"Well now, that's right pert, Marshal," Bee stated flatly. "Don't tell me you've come with arrest warrants?"

"No, not this time," Canton chimed in. He didn't care for none of the Dunns, and some of them he cared for even less.

"Come to ask you to be on the scout for Bill Doolin," Heck said. "Suspect he might return up in this neck of the woods seeing as how he's got a wife and child over near Lawson."

"Why you telling us?" Bill said.

"Because the law can't be every damn where at the same time and I need eyes on Doolin case he comes back. You got eyes, don't you?"

The Dunn Brothers looked at each other with smirks.

"Yeah, we got a shit load of eyes, Marshal. But what's in it for us?"

Canton shifted in his saddle.

"What's usually in it for you?" he said. "Reward money, if you spot him and tell us?"

"Why wouldn't we just kill him ourselves?" Bill Dunn said. "Like we did Bitter Creek and Charlie Pierce?"

Heck leveled his gaze at the eldest brother but his message was meant for all of them:

"Because you probably don't have the balls," he said. "Doolin's a sight more to deal with than either Charlie or Newcomb, else we'd probably already have had him."

"Shit," Bee Dunn said, and leaned and spat into the dirt.

"How much reward's on his head?" Bill wanted to know.

"Currently there's five thousand," Canton said.

Then there was nothing more to say and the brothers watched the trio of lawmen ride off.

"You know, Rose is shacked with that blacksmith who lives across the road from Doolin's wife's pap," Bill said.

It was true. Rose had not lingered long, had not worn mourning black but a day upon Bitter Creek's murder. Had not so much as even accused her brothers of murder and ranted and raved like a mad woman.

What she said was, "How much reward they pay you to kill my lover man?"

Bill cut her a share of the money, said, "Buy you some pretties and be glad you're shed of ol' Bitter Creek Newcomb. He was bound to come to a bad end and could have taken you with him. 'Sides, little sister, he was too old for you and cheating with whores ever chance he got."

Dal, who had unspeakable desires for his sister, confirmed

the portrait of the no-good unfaithful Newcomb, said, "I bet he gave you the pox, didn't he?"

She denied it, but secretly worried that he might have.

They had given her Newcomb's horse and saddle as well as a cut of the reward money if she backed their version of the killing, that Newcomb and Pierce had threatened them and that they had no choice but to defend themselves.

At first Rose refused to go along, but Bill reasoned to her, "Look, little sister, Newcomb's already dead. Ain't nothing any of us can do to bring him back. We might as well profit off it. Hell, there's plenty of other men who'd crawl on their knees to please you, pert as you are."

She was not a deep thinker, that they all knew. She wasn't even wily like them. Hell she was just a child, still. It didn't take much more convincing, especially when Bill took forty dollars out of the butcher cash box and handed it to her and said, "This is just an advance until we collect the rewards."

It was only two days later that she'd gone into Lawson to buy herself some of those "pretties" that Bill had suggested. Newcomb's blood bay needed a shoe on its right back foot and she'd stopped at the blacksmith's.

Tom Noble was a handsome devil with bare arms knotted with bulging muscles as he worked the forge and hammered hot steel into shape.

Like his work, he was all smoldering, sweat glistening on his hard features. With his dark moustaches he reminded Rose a little of Newcomb, only younger.

"Howdy, Little Miss," he said, wiping his forehead with a rag he took from his back pocket.

That was the start of it. He could see right away a girl wanting something more than just a shoe for her bloodbay horse. He could see luminous eyes like twin pools of blue-gray water that invited a fellow to take a dip and cool off. He could see a petulant mouth that begged for kisses, and small hard breasts rounded under her blouse. He could see how she walked off once he took in her horse, as though she knew he was watching her and wanted to show him she wasn't just some innocent little fool of a girl.

He said to himself as she crossed the street to the mercantile, "Jesus Christ" and rubbed himself through the leather apron. "Now ain't that some fine little piece" and right away began to formulate a plan to spark her.

It did not take long to bed the slip of girl who said her name was Rose Dunn and said, "Some call me the Rose of the Cimarron."

She said it while they were in bed together that first time, while his big rough hands traveled over her girl-like body.

"I bet they do," he said.

Then she told him who her brothers were and he said, "I heard of them. I sure as hell hope they won't begrudge me the pleasure of you, Rose of Cimarron."

"They killed my last beau," she said, then giggled when he practically jumped out of bed. "I suppose you heard of him too, George Bitter Creek Newcomb."

"Jesus Christ," he cursed, as if those were the only curse words he knew he used them so often.

"Shot him for the reward money," she said as she straddled him like he was a horse she intended to ride to the river. "I doubt they'd shoot you unless there was some reward money on your head."

"Goddamn" was the other epithet he often used.

"Oh, don't worry," she said, looking down at him, her long russet hair falling over her face, brushing against his chest. "I can handle my brothers."

"Oh, fuck."

"Yes, that's right," she murmured. "Let's."

It wasn't too very long before she had gathered her personal things from the ranch and moved into Tom Noble's place—a two-room house attached to his blacksmith shop, just down the street from an ice cream parlor where he sometimes took her in the evenings because he valued the cold sweetness of ice cream after a day of hammering hot steel.

During the long nights of their lovemaking she would tell him stories about her time with Newcomb, how she'd do things for him and the gang—run messages back and forth, stash guns at various hideouts, cook and clean for them.

"I was practically one of them myself," she bragged. "Heck, I bet you heard of Little Britches and Cattle Annie, ain't you?"

"Sure," he said.

"Well, I did things just as bad as any of them did. Only I never got arrested and sent away to reformatory. George said I'd make a real good outlaw someday when I growed up."

He didn't much care to hear the details of her and Newcomb's intimacies. Said, "You can leave some of that out, you know."

"Why I don't see why you'd be jealous, Tom. George is dead and it's you I'm with now."

The worst was when she said he wasn't as big down there as Newcomb was. But added, "That's all right, it don't bother me that you ain't."

"The thought of you with another man," he said, "even a dead man . . ."

She laughed at this, uproariously.

"Why Tom, I wouldn't diddle no dead man!"

"I meant . . . I mean . . ." He stammered, trying to explain what he meant, but she'd reached for him and caused him to forget everything.

Some of his friends teased him about the girl, her age.

The other thing that bothered him was how she seemed to get so sexually agitated when she talked about the bravado of not only Newcomb, but men like Pierce, and Red Buck Weightman, and most of all Bill Doolin.

"Bill Doolin's the bravest man I ever met," she said on more than one occasion. "The laws will never take him. Why, just about his entire gang has been rubbed out, but not Bill. I do believe if Bill had ever asked me to leave George and run off with him, I would have. But Bill's married and true to his wife."

She even bragged on her brothers, how manly they were.

"You want to know something?" she said one night while they were in bed, rain rattling against the windows and spilling off the roof. "My own brother, Dal, wants to have relations with me."

She didn't say it like it was a horrible thing. She said it like she was proud of the fact. She said it stroking him. She said it with the sound in her voice as if she was smoking opium. Dream-like.

She was all in all, Tom Noble thought, *a troubled child with a troubled past.* But she could have been the Devil incarnate as far as he was concerned, for she was the sultriest female in all the territory and she fucked him near to death every time.

She was gone off somewhere when the Dunn Brothers—three of them, Bill, Dal, and Bee—rode up one airless hot afternoon. They dismounted and came and stood in the shade of the lean to where Tom had his forge.

"How you and our little sister getting on?" Bill asked. They were all three armed with revolvers riding their hips. Tom wasn't at all sure if they had come to kill him.

"Fine," he said, one hand on the handle of the bellows.

"She seems fat and sassy," Bee said. "Sure enough."

Dal did not speak and Tom remembered what Rose had said

about him wanting to have relations with her and it put a knot in his stomach to see him standing there now. Goddamn he thought, a brother wanting to diddle his own sister.

"How can I help you?" Tom said.

Bill half turned and looked at the house across the street.

"Doolin's wife and father-in-law still living over there?"

"Far as I know they are. They kinda keep pretty much to themselves. I heard the old man is dying. I imagine she's taking care of him, nursing him."

"I don't suppose you've seen any sign of Bill Doolin hanging around?"

"No."

"He's got a hell of a price on his head," Bee said picking up a horseshoe from a box of them.

"That's what I understand," Tom said.

"Here's the deal," Bill said and explained to Tom about what Heck Thomas had said about keeping an eye out for any sign of Doolin.

Tom listened with interest.

"So let's say if you was to see him coming or going, you'd get on your horse and ride over to Pawnee and tell us and we'd come and shoot that son of a bitch and collect the reward, and of course, cut you in on it. How's that sound?"

"Sounds sweet as a can of peaches," Tom said.

"You keep this to yourself," Dal said, "otherwise it's no good."

"I understand."

"You come right away, you hear?" Bill said.

"Yes."

Then they mounted and rode off.

Shit, why would I share any goddamn reward with those sons a bitches? He thought. *I'll kill that bastard myself and get all the money.*

That night it was his turn to ride Rose like she was a pony at the county fair.

"What's got into you?" she said. "Why you acting like you want to kill me 'stead of fucken me?"

"Hell," he said. "I'm just feeling like the good times are coming," he said. "Now shut the hell up and give me what I come for."

She thought he'd gotten into the absinthe over at Farraday's, he was acting so crazy.

Men, she thought as he rutted over her. *What the hell is wrong with them sometimes?*

CHAPTER 38

Edith heard a noise that startled her awake. Perhaps her father had tumbled from his bed.

She lay a moment more listening. Then heard the crunch of a step upon the caliche outside her window. Her heart's beat quickened like a frightened rabbit.

"Who's there?" she whispered so faintly even she couldn't be sure she'd said it.

A tap, tap, at the window pane. She was afraid to look. Guessed it to be the midnight hour when all decent and goodly folks were abed. She reached for the gun Doolin advocated she always keep on the nightstand.

Again the light tapping. Her hand touched the cold curve of metal. She hesitated to take it fully in hand for fear it might go off.

Because of the day's heat she'd left the window slightly ajar. She feared now that whoever it was might simply climb into the bedroom.

"Don't," she said in a harsh whisper. "I have a gun."

A fleeting moment of silence, then: "Lord, honey, don't shoot your husband or I've made the trip for nothing."

She turned and pressed her face to the glass and saw Doolin staring back at her a wide grin of white teeth through his midnight beard.

"Open up," he said, "and let a poor weary traveler in."

In a moment more they were hugging, kissing, Bill smelling

like horse and cookfire and old sweat, though she did not mind, for her husband was home once more, safe and sound.

She wept warm tears against his neck.

"Hush, hush, sweet darling, no need to cry," he said.

"I'm just so happy to see you."

"I couldn't stay away no longer."

"Oh, Bill, the laws have come looking for you, asking me all sorts of questions, implying that . . ."

He placed his fingers to her lips.

"Let's not talk right now. I could use some washing up and a warm bed, and of course this."

She went and got a pan of warm water and a wash cloth and brought it to him and watched him wash, shirtless there in the small room full of glowing light from the lamp she'd lit just to see that it was really him.

"Where have you been all this time?" she asked.

"Went down to see an old pal, down in New Mexico," he said, scrubbing behind his ears then under his arms. "Figured it was safe being that far away."

"You could have sent for me," she said.

He half turned and looked at her there on the bed.

"I couldn't take the chance that the laws wouldn't follow you."

She heard her father's ragged voice calling from his bedroom and told Doolin she'd be right back.

By the time she returned Doolin was in the bed covered with a sheet. His beard and hair needed trimming and he'd lost a good deal of weight, but otherwise he was as handsome to her as ever.

"Come," he said, holding forth a hand.

She slid in next to him and nestled into the crook of his arm.

"You don't know how I craved you," he said.

"Turn out the light, Bill. You know how shy I am."

He turned out the light then removed her gown up over her head and whispered, "God, I really did miss this."

Tom Noble had risen to get a drink of water. He was a mouth breather and his throat was dry as sand. He could make his way around in the dark of his place out of familiarity, and went to the dry sink and found his tin cup and pumped the handle on the pump until cold ground water gushed forth.

He saw a light on briefly across the way. Watched it until it went out. Odd, he thought, a light on in the Ellsworth place. He thought at first maybe the old man had passed and hence a light on at this late hour.

Rose was asleep in the bed still. Gal slept like a stone. She could be getting raped by fifty Indians and wouldn't know it when she slept, he often mused.

He watched the place a bit longer as he stood drinking his cup of water. He kept thinking about that reward money. Thought, hell, it's worth a closer look, and went and slipped on a pair of trousers and left out of the house and slipped across the road.

Sure enough there was a sweated horse in the barn. Now ain't that interesting? Could be Doolin's horse, he told himself. Figured it might be, for who else would come at the midnight hour and slip into Doolin's wife's house?

He eased back out of the barn because it dawned on him that maybe Doolin was right there in the barn, hiding in the shadows, his gun drawn.

He was so nervous by the time he slipped in next to Rose he couldn't lay still.

Jeez Christ, he thought. Jeez Christ!

All the next day he kept an eye on the Ellsworth place but didn't see any trace of Bill Doolin. Maybe he had been wrong.

That evening after supper he stood looking out the window.

"What's wrong with you?" Rose asked.

"Nothing that getting rich wouldn't cure," he replied.

"You are a damn fool," she said.

"And you are awfully damn mouthy for a sprite of a girl."

"You don't like it, I'm sure I'll find someone who does."

She knew how to put the knife in where it hurt most.

"It'd be easier to give up whiskey than you," he'd told her on many occasions.

She went on to bed, he stayed at the window. Then he saw a shadow coming out of the house and go into the barn and told himself without proof, "That's him. That's Bill Doolin. I'm a son of a bitch! It's him."

He watched until the man came out of the barn leading a saddle horse, then mount it and ride away at a walk, as likely so not to disturb anybody.

The blacksmith quickly formed a plan. Loaded his Winchester rifle and went out and sat on the porch with it laid across his knees. When he comes back I'm going to empty him out of the saddle and claim that goddamn reward for myself.

He sat and sat.

Something shook him awake. It was Rose. It was full-on daylight.

"What are you doing setting out here with that gun?" she said.

He cursed himself for having fallen asleep. Couldn't know if Doolin had returned to the house or not.

"Shit," he said.

She shook her head and went back inside.

Over the next week the blacksmith ran through his mind places where he might ambush the outlaw and determined that there was one place in the direction he had seen the outlaw take on several occasions that might be the perfect spot—beneath the

Eagle Creek Bridge west of town.

So the next time he saw Doolin leave out he followed at a goodly distance until he came to the bridge then hid himself and his horse beneath it. The mosquitoes near ate him alive. He cursed them and slapped himself almost silly till daylight ran clear and clean along the land like yellow water flowing to some great unseen sea.

The smith thought, *I don't know how them goddamn law dogs do it,* his face and hands and neck stippled with mosquito bites he knew would itch like a son of a bitch for a week. But he kept imagining what he'd do with that reward money, how he and Rose would go somewhere and stay in fancy hotels and eat oysters and fuck like cats in heat all the day long.

Midmorning he heard the clop of a horse coming up the road toward the bridge. He peeked out and sure enough it was Doolin coming at a leisurely pace, could tell it was that same horse he'd examined in Ellsworth's barn. Tom Noble jacked the lever on his Winchester and waited, figured to let Doolin cross the bridge then pop up and shoot him in the back, not give him a chance.

Waited holding his breath until he heard the horse's hooves on the bridge's planking. But then halfway across the animal stopped.

Oh Jesus, oh, Jesus, Tom Noble thought. *He knows I'm down here. He's gone a kill me for sure.*

A moment passed and then another and still the horse did not move nor was there anything said by its rider.

Tom Noble was so frightened he nearly dropped the Winchester. Sweat trickled down into his eyes, causing him to blink. He was most miserable.

Then the horse at last started up and finished crossing the bridge and went on. Tom Noble was too afraid to even sneak a peek. He just sat there breathing hard trying to calm his heart.

Two opportunities and two failures.

Tom Noble figured he'd had enough trying to collect that damn reward money all for himself.

Fuck it. Let the laws catch him and split some of it with me, he thought and gladly rode on back to Lawson.

"You look like you got the measles," Rose said. "Where the hell you been all night?"

"In the weeds lying with fat whores," he said sourly.

She laughed and laughed.

"You damn idjit," she said.

And laughed and laughed.

Chapter 39

Rain fell straight down like a storm of needles. It prickled the skin.

Tom Noble came to my place, his hat crushed down and sopping wet and said, "I reckon that reward money is still good on Doolin, ain't it?"

"Well, far as I know he ain't caught yet," I said.

Tom looked hangdog whipped and said he was soaked to the bone and I told him to wait there on the porch I'd go and pour him a cup of coffee and the damn fool asked what kind was it, Arbuckle or Maxwell House. I said did it make a damn bit of difference as long as it was hot, and he said, No, he reckoned not.

So I went in and poured a cup of Mattie's coffee and brought it to him out on the porch and said, "You got some news on Doolin you wish to tell me?"

"Yes," he said. "But I need your assurance I will get my cut of the reward money."

"Quit dawdling," I warned. "If you know where he is, you best tell me."

He took his sweet time but finally said, "He's been coming and going from old man Ellsworth's place. Not only that, but sometimes he has three or four others with him. Not always, but sometimes."

"You recognize any of them?" I asked.

"Couldn't say for sure."

I asked Tom Noble when was the last time he saw him there and he said it was two or three days previous.

"All right then," I said. "Best you keep this to yourself so's not to

spook him off."

He squinched up his face and said, "You mean so's not so many others gets in on the reward by maybe killing ol' Doolin first, don't you?"

"Think what you will, you damn idiot," I said.

Soon as he left I went and got Albert and said, "Come'n, I got a line of where Doolin is."

Albert seemed excited that we might finally catch him and he would be in on it. I had to let him know it was going to take more than just the two of us, that I intended on deputizing the Dunn brothers, bloodletters that they were. I also wired a colored deputy I knew and trusted in the extreme, Rufus Cannon, to come and meet us at the Cimarron River along the west road out of Lawson, there at the Eagle Creek Bridge. I figured eight good men with guns should be enough. Maybe. Too many and it could be a disaster with everybody shooting everybody.

So we rode out to the Dunn brothers' place and announced my reason for being there and asked if they were willing to be deputized. Dal said as long as there was reward money in it and the rest agreed.

I told them to come on with us then and inside of an hour we were headed toward Lawson.

It had stopped raining just after noon and the sun came out hotter than ever, causing steam to rise off the road. We went along in silence except for the jingle of horse bit and the creaking of saddle leather.

We arrived that evening at the Eagle Creek Bridge and waited for Deputy Cannon.

He was a big man who always made the horse he was riding look too small. Bee Dunn said, "How many fuckin' shooters you got in on this, Heck? Why the rewards will be down to pocket change any more's coming."

I told him I didn't intend this on becoming a fiasco like Ingalls and that we would get Doolin or it would be a miracle if we didn't.

We rode on toward Lawson until we got to within several hundred yards of old man Ellsworth's place.

I stationed Albert along with Deputy Cannon to guard the north road. I had two of the Dunn brothers watch the east road, while me and Bee Dunn took up a position on the west road. It was by then about eight o'clock in the evening and not fully dark as of yet.

The air was oppressively warm and still.

I watched the house through a pair of field glasses and for a time I saw nothing move within or without. There were lights on inside but no movement was I able to see.

Bee Dunn said, "You think he's in there?"

"I reckon we'll find out," I said.

Bee seemed anxious to kill something with the eight-gauge shotgun he'd brought along. I had a twelve-gauge myself, a coach gun I'd taken off a prisoner I'd captured once. In testing it out a time or two, I could sweep a coyote off its feet at better than fifty yards.

Time ticked away slowly.

Bill finished his supper of fried ham and boiled potatoes, green beans cooked in bacon fat, clabber biscuits with butter and clover honey, and black coffee. Sat for a moment looking across at Edith.

"Mighty fine supper, old gal," he said with a smile.

"Why, thank you," she replied.

"I got to go out tonight," he said.

"Whatever for?"

He merely looked at her.

"You know better than to ask me," he said.

She lowered her eyes as if having been scolded.

"I was just worried in case something happened to father tonight—how I might let you know."

He wiped his bearded mouth with one of the cloth napkins and said, "I won't be gone that long. Be back before daylight."

She nodded.

He stood away from the table, came around and bent and kissed the top of her head.

"It won't be much longer and we'll be moved away from here, someplace so far away we won't ever have to worry again. Why, we'll become respectable citizens. I might even open a store that sells ladies' hats," he teased.

To this she said nothing. She'd heard so many promises before that she refused to allow herself to believe anything until it happened, though she desperately wanted to.

She reached up and patted the hand he'd put on her shoulder.

"You be careful, honey," she said.

"You know me," he said in a jolly enough mood as he went to the door and took his hat down off a peg and settled it on his head then reached for the Winchester leaning against the wall.

She dreaded seeing him with it.

"See you real soon," he said as a final farewell.

She did not go to the door nor stand from the table. She'd watched him go off too often.

"Something's moving," Heck Thomas said to Bee Dunn.

Bee strained his eyes to see as the evening pressed in on the world and the darkness began to swallow the light.

"There," Heck pointed, lowering the field glasses and handing them to Bee.

Bee did his ablest best to see what it was but he was a man with genetically poor eyesight not helped any by all the cheap whiskey he'd drank over the years nor the case of pox he suffered from.

Heck saw the shadow of a man come from the house and go into the barn.

"I can't see nothing," Bee whispered.

"Hesh," the lawman warned.

They squatted there on their bootheels both of them armed with shotguns, Bee's an eight gauge and Heck's a twelve gauge.

In a few moments a man came out of the barn leading a saddle horse by the reins. It looked too like he was carrying a rifle in his hand.

"You think that's him?" Bee whispered.

"Can't tell yet. Let him get closer."

The man walked right toward them.

Heck Thomas stood and called, "Bill Doolin, halt and throw up your hands!"

It was the only way, the lawman figured, to be certain whether it was or was not the outlaw.

Doolin dropped the reins of his horse and jacked a shell in his Winchester.

Heck had already had his shotgun barrels leveled at the man and cut loose.

A sound louder than a thunderclap shook the night, rolled and faded into silence.

Bee Dunn hadn't even attempted to take a shot. Before he realized it Bill Doolin had been swept off his feet and lay boots up in the damp grass.

"You got him!" Dunn shouted.

"I reckon I did," Heck Thomas said. "I reckon I did."

Within the house the explosion caused Edith Doolin to jump but she did not stand nor go to the door and look out.

She knew

She knew.

Chapter 40

A noise awakes her and she turns to see the shadow of a man standing in her bedroom door. The light she has left burning for him casts a soft yellow glow, framing him from rearward.

"Heck?" she says.

He steps further into the room, his slicker still dripping rain. Seems all it's done lately is rain and it is still, for it has rattled on the metal roof for three nights running.

She watches as he shucks out of it and comes and sits on the side of the bed.

"I'm so glad you're home," she says. "I always worry you won't come back to me."

"I don't mean to cause you to worry," he says and touches her cheek with a callused hand.

And for a moment there is just the sound of the rain in the room and then he says softly, "Somewhere tonight there is a new widow crying, but it isn't you. It isn't you."

ABOUT THE AUTHOR

Bill Brooks is the author of 30 novels of historical fiction, including *The Stone Garden: The Epic Life of Billy the Kid,* selected by *Booklist* as one of the ten best westerns of the past decade. Bill began writing full time with the ideal of becoming published after he ran out of other things to do when he left the health care field at the ripe old age of forty-five. He had always read that for writers "Write what you know about." Bill loved the west and anything historical including the "gangster era" of the 1930s, a period in which he wrote two novels: *Bonnie & Clyde: A Love Story* and *Pretty Boy, The Epic Life of Pretty Boy Floyd.*

Bill's westerns have been praised by *Booklist, Kirkus Review,* and *Publishers Weekly.* His John Henry Cole series has been well received and he continues to write from his home in Indiana.